Camp Club Girls

Sydney and the
Wisconsin Whispering
Woods

Cover design: Thinkpen Design

Published by Barbour Publishing, Inc., P.O. Box 719, Uhrichsville, Ohio 44683, www.barbourbooks.com

Our mission is to publish and distribute inspirational products offering exceptional value and biblical encouragement to the masses.

 Member of the Evangelical Christian Publishers Association

Printed in the United States of America.

Dickinson Press Inc., Grand Rapids, MI 49512; December 2010; D10002608

Camp Club Girls

Sydney and the
Wisconsin Whispering
Woods

Jean Fischer

BARBOUR
PUBLISHING

CHAPTER 1

Things that Go Bump in the Night

"Look out!" Sydney Lincoln screamed.

Screeeeeeech!

The wailing of tires sliding on concrete echoed in her ears. A chill raced down Sydney's spine as Aunt Dee pulled the SUV onto the shoulder of the road.

"You almost hit that thing," Sydney gasped. "What was it?"

Alexis Howell sat in the backseat. Her hands gripped Sydney's headrest.

"It ran so fast I didn't get a good look at it. I saw something big and brown. A bear, maybe?" she said.

"A deer," said Aunt Dee. "It was a huge buck. Is everyone all right?"

Alexis checked on Biscuit, also known as Biscuit the Wonder Dog. He stood in his kennel cage in the back of the SUV. "Biscuit looks a little scared, but he's fine," she said.

Aunt Dee took a deep breath and pulled back onto the narrow woodland road.

Sydney had never seen a darker summer night. The moon and the stars were trapped under clouds behind hundreds of towering pine trees. As the three—and Biscuit—traveled along, they saw animal eyes peering out at them from the forest, reflected in the beams of the headlights.

"I think we're lost," Aunt Dee announced.

"Wonderful!" Sydney sighed. "It's almost midnight, and we're lost in the middle of a national forest."

"We're not in the *middle* of the forest," said Aunt Dee. "We're barely on the edge of it. And we're not *lost* lost. I know the resort is on this road, but in the dark I'm not sure exactly where it is."

Sydney put her window down. "You can turn off the air conditioning. It's nice outside."

Aunt Dee flipped a switch on the dashboard, and the cool air stopped rushing from the vents. Just then, an awful smell filled the car.

"Skunk!" Sydney cried, quickly putting up the window.

"Eeeewwwww!" Alexis complained. "That's nasty. Did you see it?"

Sydney held her nose and flipped on the AC.

"I saw it lying dead on the road back there," said Aunt Dee.

"The poor little thing," Alexis said. "It died just trying to cross the street."

Sydney's aunt eased her foot off the accelerator, and the SUV slowed to a crawl. "Look for a long driveway to the right with a sign that says MILLER'S RESORT. It leads to the cabins and the lake."

"I think we passed it," Sydney said in a muffled voice.

She still had her hands cupped over her face to block the skunk smell.

"What?" Aunt Dee said.

"About a half an hour ago," Sydney answered. "I saw a sign that said MILLER'S RESORT with an arrow pointing to the right. I would have said something, but I didn't know we were going there."

Aunt Dee pulled the SUV to the side of the road. "How in the world did I miss it?" She made a U-turn and headed in the opposite direction. "I guess we're all tired."

The long trip was almost over. The day before, Aunt Dee and Sydney had driven eleven hours from Washington DC to Chicago, Illinois. They had dinner there with Bailey Chang and her family, who came from Peoria to see them.

Then they spent the night in a motel and, this morning, they went to the Chicago Airport to pick up Alexis. Her plane, due to arrive at one, was three hours late. They didn't leave Chicago until almost five, and for the last six hours, they had been on the road driving from Chicago to northern Wisconsin.

"I can't wait to climb into bed and go to sleep," said Sydney. "Yesterday morning, I thought a road trip was a cool idea. Now, I can't think of anything I'd like better than to get out of this SUV."

Ruff!

"Biscuit agrees," said Alexis. "He's *such* a good boy. Aren't you, Biscuit?"

7

The little dog perked up his ears and stuck one front paw through the bars of his kennel. Alexis reached back and held it. "It's probably not safe to walk in the forest at night. I mean, with bears and stuff around here."

After they backtracked several miles, Aunt Dee slowed down to make sure they wouldn't miss the sign again. "It should be on the left," she said.

"Oh my goodness!" Aunt Dee slammed on the brakes sending the girls flying against their seatbelts.

Sydney gasped. "A wolf!"

"No. That's a coyote," Aunt Dee said.

A large dog-like animal stood in the road in front of the SUV. It had big pointed ears, long legs, and a silver-brown coat. Frozen like a statue, it stared at them.

Ruff! Ruff! Ar-roof! Ruff! Ruff! Ar-roof! Biscuit barked wildly.

When the coyote heard Biscuit bark, the corners of its mouth turned up in a sneer. It showed its fangs, daring the SUV to come any closer.

"Biscuit, be quiet!" both girls exclaimed.

"Are all the windows shut?" Aunt Dee asked.

"They are," said Alexis, double-checking. She reached back and made sure Biscuit's kennel was latched.

"Look!" said Sydney, pointing to the side of the road.

Three coyote pups came out of the woods. Their mother yipped at them, and they quickly ran to her side. With a firm nudge of her nose, she sent them running.

Then she trotted after them across the road.

"I've seen more wild animals in the last half hour than I have in my whole entire life," said Alexis.

"Isn't it cool?" Sydney asked.

"Way cool," her friend answered. "But, as much as I like animals, I'm afraid of bears. That's about the only thing we haven't seen so far, and I hope we don't run into any."

A soft, little *Ruff!* came from inside the kennel cage.

They drove another quarter of a mile before they saw the sign:

MILLER'S RESORT
LAKESIDE CABINS
OPEN ALL YEAR

"We're here," said Aunt Dee. She turned the SUV onto the long, winding driveway. "I can't wait to get some sleep. I have to be at the ranger's station at nine tomorrow morning."

Sydney's aunt was a forest ranger with the National Park Service in Washington DC. For as long as Sydney could remember, Aunt Dee had worked at the many landmarks and memorials in Washington. But now she wanted to try something new. She planned to interview for a ranger job at the Chequamegon-Nicolet National Forest in Wisconsin, and she had invited Sydney and her friend, Alexis, to come along and spend a week with her in the Northwoods.

Though Sydney was from Washington DC and Alexis was from California, the two girls had met at camp. The six girls in their cabin had solved a mystery together. Dubbing themselves the Camp Club Girls, though all of the six lived in different parts of the country and were different ages, they were all great friends. And they all worked together to solve mysteries.

"We need to check in at the resort office," said Aunt Dee. "Mrs. Miller promised to stay there until we arrive." She parked the SUV in front of a two-story, white cottage and shut off the engine. A red fluorescent sign above the door flickered OFFICE, and several bright outdoor lights lit the grounds. When they opened the car doors, they felt a blast of cool, woodland air.

"I'll let Biscuit out," said Sydney.

"Wait," Aunt Dee told her. "It's not safe for him to run around here in the dark."

Biscuit lay down in his cage and sighed.

"It'll only take a minute," said Aunt Dee as they walked up the steps and onto the wide front porch. A ragged, old note was taped above the doorbell. RING AFTER 9 PM. Aunt Dee pressed the button and waited.

After a few seconds, the door swung open. A short, round lady greeted them with a smile. She wore faded blue jeans, a white tee shirt, and a yellow baseball cap that said GREEN BAY PACKERS. "Miss Powers?" she asked.

"Yes," Aunt Dee agreed, stepping inside. "We're so glad

to finally be here."

"You had a long drive," said Mrs. Miller. She walked toward the registration desk. "Come inside, girls, and shut the door behind you."

Sydney and Alexis entered the office and closed the door. A small television on a shelf behind the desk was tuned to a home shopping station.

"This is my niece, Sydney Lincoln," said Aunt Dee, wrapping her arm around Sydney's shoulder. "And her friend, Alexis Howell, from Sacramento, California."

Alexis smiled shyly.

"Goodness, all the way from Sacramento, are you?" Mrs. Miller said. "So, what do you think of the Northwoods?"

"From what I could see in the dark, it's very nice," Alexis said politely.

"So, there will be three of you, then, staying in Cabin One?" asked Mrs. Miller getting out the guest register.

"Right. Three of us," Aunt Dee said.

"We have a little dog, too," Sydney added. "Is that okay? We're taking care of him while our friend Kate is on vacation."

"We thought he'd enjoy spending time near the lake and the woods," Alexis added. "We found him when we were at Discovery Lake Summer Camp, and Kate adopted him."

Mrs. Miller opened the big registration book and asked Aunt Dee to sign her name. "Your aunt told me about the

11

dog when she made the reservations. It's okay, as long as you don't let him run around and bother the other visitors."

"We'll keep an eye on him," Sydney promised.

"And be sure to put him on a leash after dark, and stay with him when you let him out to do his business at night," Mrs. Miller warned. "Some of the wild animals around here would hurt a friendly little dog."

"Are there bears?" Alexis asked.

"Oh yeah," said Mrs. Miller. "We have black bears here. Sometimes, they wander over by the cabins at night. But, if you don't bother them, they won't bother you. And make sure you don't leave any food outside. That's how most problems between people and bears start."

Alexis shivered.

Mrs. Miller took a set of keys from a wall behind the desk. "Here are your keys," she said. "Go to the end of the driveway. It's the first log cabin on your left, the one with the big front porch. You can park behind it to unload. Then move your car back here to the parking lot. Try to be quiet. Cabin Two is occupied, and the folks are asleep."

"We will," said Aunt Dee. "And thanks for staying up for us."

"No problem," said Mrs. Miller. "Enjoy your stay. My husband and I are here if you need anything. Good night, girls. Sleep tight."

"Good night," Sydney and Alexis answered.

"Oh," said Mrs. Miller, remembering something. "And

do you have a flashlight?"

"I do," Aunt Dee replied.

"You'll need it, then, to find your way. I put a couple more in the cabin on the table."

"Thanks," said Aunt Dee. She closed the door, and they got back in the SUV and headed down the driveway.

"We're almost there, Biscuit," said Alexis, reaching into the kennel. Out of the coal-black night, the headlights shone on a log cabin with a screened porch all along its front. A sign near the door said CABIN ONE.

"Oh, Biscuit will love the porch," Sydney said. "He can hang out there all day long and not have to worry about wild animals."

"Like skunks," said Alexis.

Aunt Dee parked the SUV behind the cabin and shut off the engine. While the girls unloaded the suitcases, Sydney's aunt used her flashlight to find the lock on the door. She unlocked it, pushed the door open, and fumbled for a light switch.

When she flipped it, thankfully, the light came on. The door opened into a quaint, little kitchen that had ruffled curtains on the windows and a flowered plastic tablecloth on the small, round table. Two flashlights lay on the table with a brochure that said MILLER'S RESORT—REST AND RECREATION. Gratefully, Sydney and Alexis plopped their bags onto the floor.

"I'll let Biscuit out," said Sydney.

"Remember the leash," Alexis reminded her.

Sydney found Biscuit's leash near his kennel. Carefully, she opened the kennel door and snapped the leash onto his collar. The happy little dog came bounding out of his cage and ran circles around Sydney. Then he stopped. He put his head up and sniffed the air. He sniffed it again and let out a little *"Ruff"*

"What's the matter, boy? Do you see something?" Sydney asked. She looked toward the lake, but in the darkness, she couldn't see a thing.

Biscuit pulled hard on the leash and started to pant. He reared up on his hind legs. *Ruff! Ruff! Ar-roof! Ruff! Ruff! Ar-roof!*

"Quiet!" Sydney whispered. She thought she heard a bump. *Something's out there in the darkness*, she thought. *I'm almost sure of it.*

Just the idea that something or someone might be watching made Sydney nervous. "Come on, boy," she said, leading Biscuit back toward the cabin. "Do your business, so we can go inside."

Biscuit stood for a few seconds, anxiously staring into the darkness. Then, obediently, he did what Sydney asked and followed her to the cabin's back door.

"Why was Biscuit barking?" Aunt Dee asked when Sydney brought him inside.

Sydney shut the back door and flipped the deadbolt lock. "I think he saw something by the lake," she said. "I couldn't see anything. Do you know how dark it is out there? At Discovery Lake, the paths are lit at night, and we sort of know what animals are around. But this is way different—and spooky."

Alexis hauled her suitcase into the girls' bedroom. "By tomorrow night, we'll be getting used to the darkness and all the weird noises."

"You're probably right," said Sydney, picking up her suitcase and following Alexis into their room.

Alexis found a lamp on the nightstand next to the bunk beds. She turned the switch, and the room lit up. On one wall hung a brightly colored Indian trading blanket. Above the closet door, a mounted deer's head stared down at them.

"Oh, gross! I hate it when hunters display the heads of animals they've killed," said Alexis. She put her suitcase on the lower bunk and opened it.

"Get used to it," Sydney grinned. "There's a moose head in the bathroom."

"No there isn't!" Alexis exclaimed.

"There is," Sydney insisted. "Hey, which bunk do you want?"

"I'll take the top one," said Alexis. She took her pajamas and toothbrush out of her suitcase and headed for the bathroom.

"You just don't want to sleep next to the window," Sydney said, "in case a big bear comes along and peeks in at you."

"You're right," Alexis agreed. "I don't like bears."

Aunt Dee had parked the SUV in the lot and settled in to her room on the other side of the cabin. Before long, the girls snuggled into their beds, too.

"Lights out?" Sydney asked.

"Prayers first," said Alexis, pulling the cool sheet up under her chin.

"Okay. Say 'amen' when you're done," Sydney told her.

The girls prayed silently for a few minutes.

"Amen."

"And amen," Sydney echoed. Then she reached over and turned off the lamp.

The girls were almost asleep when the bedroom door swung open. A rush of air swept through the room as Biscuit scurried in and leaped onto the lower bunk, landing on Sydney's chest.

"Get down!" said Sydney.

Biscuit didn't move.

"Biscuit, don't stand on me. Lie down."

He pretended not to hear.

"Oh, I know what's wrong," Alexis said from the top bunk. "He wants his doll. He has that rag doll that he sleeps with. It's in the car."

Sydney sighed. "I forgot," she said. "I guess I'll have to go get it." She climbed out from under the covers and put on her shoes.

"Don't forget the flashlight," Alexis reminded her. "And

watch out for bears."

"Okay," Sydney said as she left the bedroom. She took one of the flashlights and the car keys from the kitchen table. Then she unlocked the back door and bravely walked up the driveway to the parking lot. She got Biscuit's doll from his kennel and headed back to the cabin.

When Sydney was almost there, she shined the flashlight toward the lake. The beam landed on a picnic table. She saw the gentle waves lapping on the shore, and then— a shadow. A mysterious hulking figure dashed from the beach and disappeared into the forest. Sydney heard whatever it was running through the edge of the woods.

Every ounce of courage drained from her body.

Something was watching her!

CHAPTER 2

Mountain Man

"Alex, are you awake?" Sydney asked, hurrying into their bedroom. "I think something is out there."

"Huh?" Alexis answered sleepily.

Biscuit grabbed his doll from Sydney's hand and wrestled it on the floor.

"I just saw someone, or something, hurry into the woods. I could only make out its shadow, but it looked tall and kind of hunched over. I could feel it watching me."

Alexis rubbed her eyes and sat with her feet dangling over the edge of her bed. "Now I'm afraid to go to sleep," she said. "Bears don't walk upright and hunched over, right?"

Sydney lay on her bed on her stomach and looked out the window. "Circus bears walk on their hind legs," she said. "And I've seen people throw marshmallows to bears at the National Zoo—when the bears stand up to catch them, they look sort of hunched over."

"Are marshmallows good for bears?" Alexis asked.

"I don't know," Sydney said. "But they like them."

Biscuit hopped onto the bed and wiggled next to

Sydney. He stuck his nose against the window screen and sniffed. "He smells something," Sydney whispered. "What is it, boy?"

Alexis and Sydney both sniffed the air.

"I don't smell anything, do you?" Alexis asked.

"Just fresh air," Sydney said. She reached over to pet Biscuit, and she noticed that his muscles were stiff. He stood at attention, focusing everything on his sense of smell. Then, he let out a low, soft growl. "Something *is* out there," said Sydney. "I'm sure of it."

Alexis climbed down from the upper bunk and lay on the bed with Sydney. With Biscuit between them, they peered out the window. The clouds had begun to break up now, and a narrow ray of moonlight cast the faintest bit of light on the grounds outside the cabin.

"I think I see something," Alexis said. "You're right. It looks big and hunchbacked, but I can't tell what it is. It's moving around by the beach. At least I think a beach is out there. Who knows in this darkness? Now it's stopping."

Sydney saw the shadow, too. "I wish I knew exactly where we are. The cabin is pretty close to the lake. When I came back with Biscuit's doll, the flashlight lit up the water and a picnic table. Hey, I think it's standing by the table."

Biscuit growled again, a low, menacing growl.

"What do you think it's doing?" asked Alexis.

"I have an idea," Sydney said, "I think it's a bear. Someone left food on the table, and it's after that. How brave are you?"

Alexis looked at her in the darkness. "Why?"

"Because I'm going to shine the flashlight out the window and see, once and for all, what's lurking around out there."

Biscuit shivered.

"Oh Syd, are you sure that's a good idea?" asked Alexis.

"We're the Camp Club Girls," Sydney answered. "Solving mysteries is what we do." She reached over to the nightstand and got the flashlight. "Are you ready?" she asked.

"I guess so," Alexis replied.

Sydney pointed the flashlight at the window and flipped the switch. "Oh!" she gasped.

Alexis caught her breath as Sydney turned off the flashlight and both girls ducked under the windowsill.

A man lurked outside, a big, burly man with a bushy brown beard and a ruddy complexion. He wore a floppy tan hat, khaki colored clothing, and brown hiking boots. In one hand, he carried a long, thick walking stick. It looked bumpy—perhaps carved out of a tree branch. A huge, bulky backpack hung over his shoulders, and attached to it was a frying pan and a bedroll. The flashlight startled him. He grabbed something from the picnic table and ran off toward the woods.

Biscuit was barking wildly when Aunt Dee rushed into their room.

"What's going on?" she asked.

"Someone is out there," Sydney said. "A guy."

"What do you mean, a guy?" Aunt Dee said, sounding concerned.

"I went to the car to get Biscuit's doll, and when I was almost back to the cabin, I saw something big hurry into the woods," said Sydney. "It looked like a bear. So, Alex and I looked out the window. We shined the flashlight outside to see if we could see anything, and we saw a guy. He looked like a mountain man. He's gone now. He ran into the woods."

Aunt Dee climbed onto the bed and looked out the window. "Was he looking in at you?"

"No," said Alexis. "I think we scared him. He was doing something at the picnic table when we turned on the flashlight, but we didn't see what. He took off running that way." She pointed.

Aunt Dee locked the window and drew the curtains closed. "Keep the window closed tonight," she said. "And Sydney, you shouldn't have gone out there alone to get Biscuit's toy."

Biscuit jumped to the floor, picked up his doll, and scampered out of the room.

"The ceiling fan should keep you cool enough," said Aunt Dee. "In the morning, we'll have a better idea of who and what you saw."

"It *is* morning!" said Sydney.

"I know." Aunt Dee sighed. "And we should all be asleep." She flipped on the ceiling fan and left the room, closing the girls' door but leaving just enough room for Biscuit to go in and out.

21

Alexis climbed the ladder to the upper bunk. "What do you think he was up to?" she asked.

"Beats me," said Sydney. "I think maybe he's camping in the woods or something. His clothes looked dirty and worn, and did you notice the bedroll?"

"I did," Alexis answered. "And the frying pan, too. Obviously, he's a camper. I'm just glad we saw a person out there instead of a big grizzly bear. A camper guy I can handle, but not a bear that wants to make a snack out of my arms or legs."

Sydney laughed. "Oh Alex, what's gotten into you? You're usually so positive."

"Not when it comes to bears," Alex said. "Unless, of course, they're in a zoo. Then I think they're cute and cuddly."

Sydney rolled onto her side and adjusted the pillow under her head. "Well, I feel safe here with the window shut and the doors to the cabin locked. Tomorrow we can look for evidence and maybe find out what our mountain man was up to. Goodnight, Alex."

"Goodnight, Syd," Alexis said. "And by the way, Wisconsin doesn't have any mountains."

"I know," Sydney said, sleepily. "But still, he looked like a mountain man."

• — • — •

In the morning, the girls awoke to the sound of sausages sizzling in a frying pan. Aunt Dee was in the kitchen making a big country-style breakfast. She was already dressed in her park ranger uniform, and when the girls came to the kitchen table still in their pj's, she scooped scrambled eggs onto their plates. "Help yourselves to some pancakes," she said. "The sausages are almost ready. I was just about to come in and wake you guys up."

Sydney yawned and put several pancakes on her plate. "Thanks for making breakfast, Aunt Dee," she said. "I'm hungry enough to eat a bear." She looked at Alexis and grinned.

"I'm not *that* hungry," Alexis said. "But I am hungry enough to eat pancakes. Thanks, Miss Powers. This is great."

Aunt Dee carried the frying pan to the table and put two sausages on each of their plates. "You're welcome," she said. "You can make supper tonight."

She set the frying pan in the sink and sat down at the table. Before they ate, they thanked God for their food.

"So, did you sleep well?" Aunt Dee asked.

"Sort of," Alexis answered.

"Me, too, sort of," Sydney added. "I dreamed about that guy we saw. Why are the drapes all shut?"

"I haven't had time to open them yet," Aunt Dee told her. "As soon as I woke up, I dressed and started breakfast. I have to leave in a few minutes for my interview."

Sydney got up and walked into the small living room. She pulled the cord that opened the drapes on the big picture window. Bright sunlight flooded the room.

Camp Club Girls

Beyond the screened porch, Sydney saw a grassy front yard. It led down a gentle slope to the lake, which was only a short distance from the cabin's front door. A very narrow strip of sandy beach stretched along the water's edge, and an aluminum rowboat lay there upside down. The water glistened in the sunlight, and a pair of ducks floated on the surface near a long, wooden dock.

"This is cool!" Sydney said. "We're closer to the water than I thought." She went back to the table and continued eating her breakfast.

"I'm sure you'll find plenty to do," Aunt Dee said. "The resort brochure tells about swimming, fishing, and rowing. A small grocery store is within walking distance—and also an ice cream and coffee shop with video games and Internet access."

"Great!" said Alexis. "Then we can e-mail our friends."

Sydney knew that Alexis referred to the other Camp Club Girls—Bailey Chang, Kate Oliver, Elizabeth Anderson, and McKenzie Phillips. Kate, the technological one, had set up a Web page with a chat room. When they weren't at camp and since they lived in different parts of the country, it was like their own private cabin in cyberspace.

"We'll e-mail them later," Sydney said. "We can tell them about the mountain man."

"And almost hitting a deer, and the skunk, and the coyote," said Alexis, before taking the last bite of her scrambled eggs.

"Maybe we should leave out the wild animals part," Sydney suggested between sips of orange juice from a red plastic cup. "Kate might worry about Biscuit."

"You're right," said Alexis. "We'll leave that part out." She reached down to pat Biscuit on his head. He sat patiently at her feet, apparently hoping she would give him a bite of sausage.

Aunt Dee gathered her purse and briefcase. She nestled her tan ranger's hat on her head and picked up her car keys. "If you need me, you know my cell phone number. And you girls stay out of trouble today," she said. "Okay?"

"Who, us? Get into trouble?" Sydney smiled.

"Listen, girlfriend," said Aunt Dee. "I haven't forgotten that you and Elizabeth got mixed up in an assassination plot to kill the president. I still have gray hairs from that little adventure."

She meant the time when Sydney and Elizabeth followed some thugs who planned to set off a bomb at Fort McHenry. Sydney saved the president's life when she grabbed the bomb and dumped it into Baltimore Harbor. An event they'd dubbed *Sydney's DC Discovery.*

"We'll be fine," Sydney promised.

Aunt Dee waved and went out the door.

The girls cleaned the table, washed the dishes, and made sure Biscuit had food and water.

"So, what do you want to do now?" Alexis asked after they got dressed.

"I don't know," said Sydney. "Let's go outside."

They put Biscuit on the big, screened porch. Then Sydney locked the door and stuck the key in the pocket of her gray sweatpants. "Let's see if the mountain man left us any clues."

The other visitors weren't up yet, and the lake was quiet. Chipmunks scampered about looking for scraps of food, seeds, and other treats. Birds scurried from the ground to the trees, feeding their babies in well-hidden nests. The girls walked to the picnic table where they'd seen the man the night before. The rickety old table held nothing more than a small pile of peanuts, obviously left by some well-meaning guest who wanted to feed the animals.

"Maybe that's what he was doing," Sydney said. "Leaving food for the critters."

She tossed a peanut on the ground. Instantly a chipmunk skittered over and popped the whole thing into its cheek. Alexis tossed another one. The girls took turns tossing peanuts until the whole pile was gone.

"I don't like the idea of someone putting food out at night," said Alexis. "It might attract bears." She sat down on the picnic bench. "Ouch!" She jumped up, rubbing her behind.

"What's wrong?" asked Sydney.

"I sat on something sharp." Alexis checked out the spot where she'd sat. "Hey, look. What are these things?"

Three tiny bunches of brightly colored feathers lay on

the ground. Each bunch was gathered tightly at the bottom with a small, sharp hook tucked inside.

"Fishing flies," said Sydney.

"Fishing what?"

"They're fishing flies," Sydney said. She picked one up and held it in her hand. "When you go fishing, you put one of these on the end of your line. When the little fishies see the colorful feathers swimming under the water, they bite. That's how you catch a fish."

"How do you know this stuff?" Alexis asked.

"My aunt's a park ranger," Sydney said. "I've been fishing lots of times."

"Hey! What are you doing with my fly?" A short, skinny, redheaded boy marched over to the picnic table. "Give it to me." He held out his hand.

Gently, Sydney placed the fly in the palm of his hand. She pointed to the others on the ground. "There's more," she said.

The boy bent and picked them up.

Sydney decided he was about the same age as she and Alexis. "Are you staying here?" Sydney asked. "We just got in last night, and we're in Cabin One. I'm Sydney, and this is Alex."

The boy scowled. "We're in Cabin Two. I need these for the fishing contest. Alex? What kind of name is that for a girl?"

"It's short for Alexis," Alex told him. She already sensed

trouble. Nothing about this boy was friendly.

"And what's your name?" Sydney asked.

"Duncan," he answered sharply.

"So what about this fishing contest, Duncan?" Sydney wondered.

"What about it?" Duncan checked the flies to make sure they weren't broken.

"You said something about a fishing contest," Sydney said. "I always like a good contest, and maybe I want to sign up."

"You can't. Girls don't fish," Duncan said matter-of-factly.

Sydney got that expression on her face, the one Alexis recognized as determination. No one, absolutely no one, ever told Sydney Lincoln that she couldn't compete. She lived for competition.

"Oh yes, girls *do* fish!" Sydney told him. "Where do I sign up?"

Duncan looked at her. The corner of his mouth turned up in a sly smile. Then he shook his head back and forth, uttered a wicked little laugh, and walked away.

"Ooooo!" Sydney said under her breath. "I don't like him. *Girls can't fish!* Who does he think he is? I'm going to find out where to sign up for that contest, and you just watch. I'm going to win that contest if it's the last thing I do!" She sighed with exasperation.

" 'A gentle answer turns away wrath, but a harsh word stirs up anger,' " said Alexis. "It's in the Bible. Proverbs 15:1."

"You sound like Elizabeth," said Sydney. Elizabeth knew

an amazing amount of scriptures. "But I'm not angry," Sydney continued. "I'm just frustrated because he thinks girls can't fish, or shouldn't fish, or whatever. Let's go to the office and find out where to sign up." She headed toward the cabins.

"Hey," said Alexis. "What's this?" She picked up a paperback book from the grass: *Field Guide to Mushrooms.*

"Keep it," Sydney said. "It might belong to the mountain man."

"And look," Alexis said. "The bottom of the rowboat is covered in wet seaweed, and the squishy mud has big footprints in it. And what are these things?" She pointed to pieces of brown, slimy fungus at the edge of the beach.

"I dunno. We'll check it out later," said Sydney. "Right now, my mind's on that contest."

Northern Lights

Mrs. Miller sat behind the registration desk drinking a cup of coffee. "Good morning, girls," she said when Sydney and Alexis entered the office. "You're up bright and early."

"Hi," said Sydney. "I have a question. Where do I sign up for the fishing contest?"

"Which one?" Mrs. Miller asked. She opened a bakery box filled with donuts and offered them to the girls.

"No thanks," Sydney said as Alexis grabbed a crème-filled, chocolate-covered long boy. "There's more than one contest?"

Alexis kept busy studying a map of the lake hanging on the wall.

"There's always fishing contests on North Twin Lake," said Mrs. Miller. "Here's a list of our current ones." She handed Sydney a flyer.

FISHING CONTESTS
August 2 through 9
Off Shore: Biggest Fish—Prize $200 and 50% Off

TAXIDERMIST SERVICES AT SCALE AND HIDE TAXIDERMY
IN EAGLE RIVER
DOCKSIDE: BIGGEST FISH—PRIZE: $100 AND
FREE ALL-YOU-CAN-EAT FISH FRY AT
CLIFF'S BOATHOUSE CAFÉ IN CONOVER

"The kid in Cabin Two, Duncan," said Sydney. "Which contest did he sign up for?"

"He probably signed up for the dockside contest," Mrs. Miller answered. "Children under 13 can only compete in offshore if they're with an adult."

Alexis walked to the desk and helped herself to another chocolate-covered donut.

"Okay, I want to sign up for dockside," said Sydney. "And Alexis does, too."

"I do?" said Alex, licking chocolate frosting from her fingers.

Mrs. Miller smiled. "Not a fisherman, are you?" she asked.

"I've fished a little," said Alexis, "but I've never fished in a contest."

"Well, you girls go up there to the end of the drive. Then you turn left and walk down the road a bit. You'll see Tompkins' Ice Cream Shop. Go inside there, and that's where you sign up. You sure you don't want a donut?" Mrs. Miller slid the box toward Sydney.

"No thank you," Sydney said again. "Come on, Alex. Let's go sign up."

The girls got Biscuit from the cabin, and Alexis made sure his leash was firmly fastened to his collar. Then the three of them headed up the drive toward the road.

Soon they came to a gas station and a row of quaint little shops. Tompkins' Ice Cream was the first two-story building on the left. A red-striped awning hung over the wide front window, and a sign in the window said:

COFFEE, REGULAR AND SPECIALTY
MUFFINS, SCONES, AND OTHER SWEETS
ICE CREAM AND FREE INTERNET ACCESS
OPEN EVERY DAY 8 TO 8

The girls opened the door and went inside.

Four small tables sat in the middle of the shop, and three huge, wooden booths lined one wall. The opposite wall had an old-fashioned soda fountain with a lunch counter and tall stools with round, red seats. The tables and booths were empty. Several men sat at the counter drinking hot coffee out of thick, black mugs.

"No dogs allowed," said a man wearing a white apron. He stood behind the counter writing the daily specials on a blackboard. "You can tie it to the hitch outside the front door."

Biscuit cocked his head and raised one paw to beg. Then he raced toward the man, pulling the leash out of Sydney's hand. He stood up with his paws against the man's knees and wagged his tail.

"There, there, now," the man said, patting Biscuit's head. "I have to kick you out, buddy—the health inspector says so."

Sydney picked up the end of Biscuit's leash and apologized. "Are you the manager?" she said as Alexis took Biscuit outside.

"I own the place," the man said.

"Where do we sign up for the fishing contest—the one on the docks?"

"Right here." The man looked past Sydney. "Are you signing up for your dad, or your brother, or someone else?"

"I'm signing up for me!" Sydney said as Alexis came back into the shop.

A man at the counter chuckled. "Girls don't fish," he said.

Sydney felt the blood rush to her face. "We do, too," she told him. "Where's the sign-up sheet?"

The owner walked to the end of the counter and came back with some papers attached to a clipboard. "Here 'tis," he said. "Do you know what you're fishing for?"

Sydney signed her name and Miller's Resort, Cabin One. "I'm fishing for the biggest fish dockside."

The man at the counter chuckled again. "What *kinds* of fish?" he asked.

Sydney had no idea what kinds of fish were in North Twin Lake, and she didn't like that the man tried to make her look stupid. "All kinds!" she replied firmly.

She handed the clipboard to Alexis. Alex hadn't

planned to compete, but when she heard the man laugh at Sydney's answer, she signed her name, too.

"May we use the computer?" she asked.

"Over there," the owner said, pointing to the corner of the room.

Sydney gave him back the clipboard. "Internet access is free, right?"

"Correct," the man said. He took a coffeepot from a heated plate behind the counter and filled the men's cups.

"Did you see that Duncan kid's name on the list?" Alexis asked as they walked to the computer.

"Yes, right at the top. He's Duncan Lumley. Age twelve."

They sat down at the computer, and Sydney typed in her name and password. Then she logged on to the Camp Club Girls Web site. Bailey was online.

> Sydney: *Hi, Bailey. Greetings from Tompkins' Ice Cream Shop in the Northwoods! Alex says hi, too. We're on the shop's computer.*
>
> Bailey: *Hi, guys! Alex, sorry I didn't get to see you when you arrived in Chicago.*
>
> Alexis: *No problem. Maybe we can meet this weekend before I catch my plane.*
>
> Sydney: *You'll never guess what we just did.*
>
> Bailey: *What?*
>
> Sydney: *Alex and I signed up for a fishing contest.*
>
> Bailey: *Get out of town! How come?*

Sydney: *An obnoxious kid named Duncan is staying at our resort. He told me this morning that girls can't fish. So we're going to show him that girls not only fish, but girls WIN fishing contests.*

Bailey: *You show him, Sydneykins. A resort? That sounds fancy.*

Alexis: *Think again. It has an office, which is an old two-story cottage, and a row of small cabins not much bigger than our cabins at camp.*

Bailey: *Cool.*

Sydney: *So, do you know much about catching fish? That kid, Duncan, is using feather flies. I don't know what he uses for bait, though. What do you think? Worms?*

Bailey: *Hang on a minute.*

"Do you want an ice-cream cone?" Alexis asked Sydney.

"Alex! You just had a big breakfast and two donuts," Sydney exclaimed. "What's up with you? You usually eat healthy."

"I know," her friend answered, "but all this fresh air makes me hungry. I'll wait. Maybe I can get an ice cream when we leave."

Bailey: *Sorry guys. I went and asked my dad what he uses for bait. He fishes all the time.*

35

He said big fish like dough balls. Take a little glob of fresh dough, mix in some tuna, and roll it in corn meal. That's the secret, he said. Put them in the fridge overnight to firm up. Make sure to stick them onto the hooks good. Otherwise, they'll fall off.

Sydney: *Tuna? That sounds like cannibalism!*

Bailey: *Fish are cannibals, Sydzie.*

Sydney: *Gross. But tell your dad thanks. Will you set up a chat with the girls for tonight at 6:30 CDT? We saw a strange guy near the cabin last night, and we want to know whether you think he's suspicious.*

Bailey: *Will do. Why do you think he's strange?*

Sydney: *He looked like a mountain man, and he ran off into the woods. We couldn't see much in the darkness.*

Bailey: *There aren't any mountains in Wisconsin, are there?*

Sydney: *I know. But that's the best way I can describe him. He looked like someone who lives alone in the mountains. Think of Heidi's grandfather, or better yet John the Baptist, the guy in the Bible who was a loner and wore clothes made of camel's hair. He stayed alive by eating locusts and wild honey.*

Bailey: *John lived in the desert, Sydz, and he was Jesus' cousin.*

Sydney: *Whatever. Just think of a big, bearded,*
lonesome guy, with a backpack and tattered
clothes.

Bailey: *OK. I'll tell the girls. We'll meet you here*
at 6:30. In the meantime, good luck with the
old man of the woods.

Sydney: *Thanks, Bailey. See you later.*

Alexis chewed a hangnail on her thumb, a bad habit she wished she didn't have.

"So, do you still want ice cream?" Sydney asked.

"No. I've changed my mind," said Alexis. "Maybe when we come back tonight. I have an idea, though."

"What's that?" said Sydney.

"There's a grocery store across the street. Let's get some frozen pizza dough and other stuff to make pizza. The dough will be thawed out by suppertime. We can make pizza tonight and keep some of the dough for bait. What do you think?"

"Great idea," said Sydney, shutting down the computer. "Let's go shopping."

"Happy fishing," the man at the lunch counter said sarcastically as the girls left the shop. Sydney and Alexis ignored him.

Biscuit sat patiently just outside the door, his leash tied to a big, iron hook screwed into the building's outer wall.

"Just a few more minutes, boy," said Alexis, petting his

fluffy fur. "We're going across the street to buy groceries. Then we'll come back to get you."

Biscuit whined softly and raised his right paw as if to say, *please don't leave me here.*

"I'm texting Aunt Dee," Sydney said as Alexis reassured Biscuit. She took out her cell phone and typed NEED LIST OF KINDS/SIZES OF FISH IN N. TWIN LAKE AND BEST WAY 2 CATCH THEM. WILL XPLAIN L8R. SYD.

"Okay, that's done. Now let's get the stuff for the dough balls."

The girls left Biscuit and crossed the street.

Sydney and Alexis loaded a large package of frozen pizza dough into their shopping cart. Then they added pepperoni, some olive oil, cornmeal, a big bag of shredded pizza cheese, and a can of tomato sauce.

"How about some mushrooms?" asked Alexis. "Do you like them on your pizza?"

"Sure," said Sydney. "And onions, too."

Alexis put a carton of mushrooms and an onion into the shopping cart. Then they headed to the checkout counter. Just as they were about to pay for their groceries, Sydney remembered something. "Where can I find canned tuna?" she asked the cashier.

"At the end of aisle ten."

Sydney hurried off and returned with three cans of tuna.

"Three!" Alexis exclaimed.

"I want to catch lots of fish," said Sydney.

They left the store carrying paper bags filled with groceries, and headed back across the street.

"Hey!" Alexis said. "Biscuit's gone!"

Biscuit's leash and collar hung from the hook, but Biscuit was nowhere in sight. The owner of Tompkins' Ice Cream Shop stood outside. "That way," he said, pointing in the direction of the resort. "He slipped out of his collar and scampered off."

Sydney shoved her grocery bags at Alexis and sprinted as fast as she could down Twin Lakes Road.

"Wow, can that girl run!" the man said.

"She did track and field in the Junior Olympics," said Alexis, taking Biscuit's leash off the hook in the wall. She dropped it and his collar into one of the grocery bags. Then she hurried after Sydney. When she got to the resort, she found her friend alone on the cabin's front porch.

"I don't know what to do," Sydney cried. "He's lost!"

A sinking feeling swept through Alexis's stomach as she put up the groceries and hung up Biscuit's collar. "We have to find him, Sydney. But where do we start to look? He could be anywhere."

Ruff-ruff! Ruff-ruff! Biscuit's bark came from far away—deep in the woods surrounding the lake. "Biscuit!" they shouted. "Biscuit! Biscuit! Here, boy!"

When Biscuit didn't come, they dashed into the forest, hurrying toward the sound of his bark.

Alexis grabbed Sydney's arm, stopping her dead in her tracks.

"What?" Sydney protested.

"We need to mark our trail," said Alexis. "Remember? We learned it in camp. If we aren't familiar with our surroundings, we should mark a trail so we can find our way back."

She found some pinecones on the path and stacked them into a neat little pyramid. Then she laid a stick next to them, pointing in the direction they'd come from. "Whenever we make a turn, we have to mark the place," she said.

The girls continued in the direction of Biscuit's barking, stopping to mark the trail every time they turned. After a while, they didn't hear his barking anymore. They only heard birds chirping loudly in the trees.

"Why do you think he stopped barking?" Sydney asked. "Or. . .do you think that someone stopped him from barking?"

"I don't know," Alexis said. "But I just said a silent prayer and asked God to keep him safe."

"I'm praying, too," said Sydney.

Tall trees blocked out most of the sunlight, and soft pine needles covered the cool forest floor. The girls looked for Biscuit's pawprints there, but found nothing.

"I hope he didn't run into a bear," said Alexis.

"I doubt it," said Sydney. "Besides, Biscuit could outrun a bear or any other wild animal. He's fast."

"I guess so," said Alexis, marking their trail with a little pile of stones.

Sydney walked on ahead of her and disappeared among the trees.

"Yeeeeeeah! No! No! Stop it!"

Alex ran toward her friend's screams. She found Sydney lying face down on the ground with her hands over her head. Biscuit licked her face with his long, pink tongue.

"Oh Biscuit!" Alexis gushed. She picked up the little dog. "Eewwwww, Biscuit. You stink!"

"I know," said Sydney, getting up and brushing herself off. "He smells awful. Biscuit, where have you been? What's all that smelly stuff in your fur?"

Biscuit let out a sad whimper. Alexis put him down, and he sat in front of her. He raised a paw.

"He came out of nowhere and ran between my legs," Sydney said. "I tripped over him and fell. Stay with him. I'm going to walk over there and see if I can find out what he got into."

Sydney wove her way through the brush and the pine trees sniffing the air for anything that smelled like Biscuit now smelled.

"Alexis, come here," she called. "I see something."

Reluctantly, Alexis picked Biscuit up and went to where Sydney was.

"Look at that," Sydney said, pointing slightly to the right.

In the distance, deep in the forest, she saw an eerie purple glow. It was the color of lilac nail polish, not a deep purple, but soft and wispy. It lit up the trees, making

41

the forest look enchanted.

"Whoa," said Alexis. "What do you think that is?"

"Should we go and check it out?" Sydney asked.

Alexis looked at Biscuit. "I don't trust him not to run again," she said. "Otherwise, I'd love to check it out. We'd better take him home."

"I guess so," said Sydney. "Unless—"

She saw a Virginia Creeper vine growing around a nearby tree trunk. She reached for it.

"Stop!" Alexis said, grabbing Sydney's hand. "It's poison ivy!"

"No, it's not. It has five leaves, not three." Sydney broke off a piece, and tied it around Biscuit's neck. "These vines are strong, and they'll make a good collar."

She broke off a longer piece and tied it to the collar like a rope. "There, now he has a leash. Oh Biscuit, you smell just terrible!"

Biscuit looked at her and sighed.

Cautiously, the girls walked through the forest toward the light.

"Maybe we're seeing the Northern Lights," Alexis suggested.

"Nice try," Sydney said. "But you can only see the Northern Lights at night."

They kept moving toward the purple glow. If they walked just a few more yards, they might discover what caused it.

WHOOOOOOSH!

Suddenly, the forest came alive. A noise surrounded them, like air rushing through a tunnel.

"Go back! Go back! Go back!"

At the sound of the loud whisper, Alexis screamed.

Sydney scooped Biscuit in her arms.

The girls ran for their lives!

Lost

"Run!" Alexis cried. "Hurry!"

The girls ran as fast as their legs could carry them. Then Sydney stopped.

"Wait," she said. She grabbed Alexis's arm. "I don't think it's following us."

Alexis quit running. She stood huffing and puffing, trying to catch her breath. Gigantic pine trees surrounded them, and she wrapped her arms around one of the trunks to brace herself.

"I can't hear it anymore," said Sydney. She set Biscuit down in a soft pile of leaves. "What do you think it was?"

"A bear, maybe?" Alexis answered.

"Bears don't glow purple and talk," Sydney said. *"Shhhhh."*

They listened. The whooshing had become a buzz, barely noticeable, locked deep inside the forest.

"Did you hear what it said?" asked Alexis. " *'Get out! Get out! Get out!'* "

"That's not what I heard," Sydney told her. "I heard *'Go*

back! Go back! Go back!' But whatever it said, something doesn't want us here."

Biscuit rolled happily in the pine needles. He didn't seem bothered by the spooky sound in the woods.

"We need to get out of here," Sydney said. She picked up the end of Biscuit's viney leash and started walking.

"Syd?" Alexis asked, "Are you sure the resort is that way?"

Sydney stopped. She looked left and right and all around. "I think we came from over there," she said, pointing to her left.

"I think it's that way," said Alexis, pointing to her right. "I didn't pay attention to where we were going when we ran away. And unless we find our trail markers, I think we're"— she hesitated—"lost."

Sydney sighed. "Okay. We've been lost in the woods before. Let's just stay calm and practice what we learned at Discovery Lake Camp."

"Well, the first thing you're supposed to do is blow a whistle," said Alexis, "which we don't have. Or shout to get someone's attention. And the last thing we want to do right now is draw attention to ourselves. Whatever is out there probably wonders where we are. So making noise is not an option."

"I'm thinking," Sydney said. "We learned at camp to look for water, like a river or stream, and follow it. That way we might run into someone canoeing, or fishing, or whatever."

Alexis started chewing her hangnail again. "That would be great except that the only water around here is the lake, and we don't know where that is right now. Besides, we don't want to run into whatever it is that's trying to get us."

"We don't know for sure that it's trying to get us," said Sydney. "What's up with you, Alex? You're always the one with the positive, realistic attitude."

"Well, I think 'go back' or 'get out' or whatever it said is enough for us to know that it doesn't want us around," Alexis argued. "Anyhow, I'm sure we can find our way home. We just need to stay calm." She looked at her watch.

"What time is it?" Sydney asked.

"Almost noon."

Sydney handed Biscuit's leash to Alexis. Then she started walking in circles around the pine trees.

"What are you doing?" Alex wondered.

"Looking for moss. It grows on the north side of tree trunks. The woods are south of the resort, so if we can find north, then we'll know which direction to go."

Biscuit decided that Sydney was playing a game. He pulled hard on his viney leash until it snapped in two. Then, joyfully, he pranced around the tree trunks with her.

Alexis busied herself with marking the spot where they were. She piled up some pine branches and laid two sticks in a criss-cross on top of them. "There," she said. "This is our starting point. If we see this again, we'll know that we're walking in circles. Why don't you just call your Aunt

Dee and tell her we're lost? You have your cell phone."

"Oh, right," Sydney complained as she inspected another trunk. "I'll call her in the middle of her interview and say, 'Aunt Dee, we're lost in the Chequamegon-Nicolet National Forest, and something wicked is in here with us. Do you think you might be able to get away for a few minutes and come find us?' "

"It was just an idea," said Alexis.

Biscuit stopped and sniffed the air. His ears perked up. He let out a little *Ar-roof*, and then off he ran into the forest.

"Oh no," said Sydney, "Not again! Let's go."

"Wait," said Alexis. "Remember what that thing said. Are you sure you want to go back in there?"

"Think about it, Alex—it's Biscuit. We *have* to go. If we lost him, Kate would never forgive us."

"She would, too," said Alexis, stalling for time. "She has to. The Bible says to."

Sydney took off after Biscuit. Reluctantly, Alexis followed. "We have to be quiet," she said. "If we start calling for him, whatever it is might hear us."

"You're right," Sydney agreed.

The buzzing noise grew louder as they approached the spot where they'd heard the *whoosh*—where the voice whispered, "Go back. Go back. Go back."

The forest seemed darker now, and they heard that noise, the persistent *buzz*, a low sound, almost a growl.

Then, as Sydney and Alexis walked deeper into the forest, they saw the eerie purple glow.

"What's that?" Sydney whispered.

"It's the purple light. We saw it before," said Alexis.

"No," said Sydney. "Something is out there walking in the woods."

The words had no sooner left her lips than they saw the mountain man. He stood in a small clearing in the distance.

"Drop!" Sydney gasped. The girls fell to the ground and hid behind a huge log.

Alexis peeked around one side of it.

"Oh my goodness!" she whispered. "He's got Biscuit!"

The mountain man walked toward them with Biscuit held firmly in the crook of his left arm. In his right hand, he carried the walking stick. The backpack was gone, but he still wore the floppy cap and ragged clothes. As he came nearer, the girls heard his deep, gruff voice.

"I need to get you back," he said. "If they come looking for you, they might find out what I'm doing. It'll be in all the newspapers and even on television. And I'm not ready for that yet."

As he got closer, Alexis and Sydney prayed that Biscuit wouldn't bark or wiggle out of the man's arms and run to them. Even a whisper could be heard, so they just huddled together behind the log and looked at one another with desperation.

Baw-waw-waw!

Suddenly, a hollow, loud barking sound came out of the eerie purple glow. It echoed through the forest and made Sydney shiver. She felt Alexis grip her forearm.

"I never tied Fang up before," said the man's rough voice. "He's not at all happy about it. Now, once I get you back home, don't you come after us again, you hear? This is no place for a friendly little dog like you. You tell that gal to keep you on your leash."

The girls heard the mountain man's boots crunch pinecones against the forest floor. He was almost to the log now, and they plastered their bodies tightly against the ground.

Please, dear God, don't let him see us, Sydney prayed silently.

Biscuit began to whine, sensing that they were nearby.

"Whoa, slow down there, boy," said the mountain man, tightening his grip. "Nothing's going to get you."

Sydney could imagine Biscuit squirming to get out of the man's arms.

"Whew!" she heard the man exclaim. "Your owner's going to be mad when she gets a whiff of you. You shouldn't have rolled in my manure pile."

Certain that the man was far enough away, Sydney let out a sigh of relief.

"He saw you!" Alexis whispered.

"No, he didn't," Sydney replied. "He walked right on by."

"I don't mean now," said Alexis. "I mean when you were

out with Biscuit last night. He said, 'Tell that gal to keep you on your leash.' "

"You're right," whispered Sydney. "So now what do we do?"

"We follow them," said Alexis.

The thing called Fang started barking again. Soon its deep *Baw-waw-waws* mixed with long, mournful *AR-ROOooooos.*

"I think he has a wolf tied up out there," said Sydney.

"Oh, do you think so?" Alexis shuddered.

"Whatever it is sounds big," Sydney replied.

They got up from the ground and followed the mountain man, making sure that they stayed well behind him and hidden in the trees.

"Do you know what?" Sydney whispered as she ducked under a low branch. "I just thought of something."

"What?" said Alexis, avoiding the same branch.

"We need to get ahead of them."

"Why?" Alexis wondered nearly tripping over a rock half buried in the soil.

"Because Biscuit is smart," Sydney said. "If we're behind them, he'll run right to us when the mountain man puts him down. Then we'll be caught for sure. And who knows what he'd do to us. Probably take us back to that purple glow where he has the wolf tied up." She squeezed around a Cockspur Hawthorne tree and caught her arm on one of its long, sharp thorns. "Ouch!" she squealed.

"Ssshhhh!" Alexis scolded.

It was too late. Biscuit heard Sydney's cry.

Ruff-ruff-aroof! Ruff-ruff-aroof!

"Oh no," said Alexis. "Dear God, please, please, let the mountain man hang on to Biscuit."

"Lord, hear our prayer," Sydney agreed, quickly wiping a dribble of blood from her arm.

They waited, expecting Biscuit to bound through the woods right to them. But nothing happened.

"Oh thank you, Lord," Sydney said.

"You're right," said Alexis as they slipped in and out among the trees. "We should get to the resort before Biscuit does. I sure wish we knew a shortcut."

"Ooof!" She tripped over something and fell flat on her face.

"Are you okay?" asked Sydney.

"I'm fine," said Alexis, pushing herself up onto her knees. "I just tripped over this. . .shovel."

A garden shovel with a long wooden handle lay in the dirt under Alexis. "This is a strange place for a shovel," she said, standing up. "Someone must have been digging here. Maybe looking for something."

"Or, maybe burying something," Sydney suggested.

The girls looked at one another. Without saying a word, each knew what the other was thinking. The shovel belonged to the mountain man.

"Hey," said Alexis, brushing dirt and pine needles off of

51

her knees. "Look!" She pointed to the base of a nearby tree trunk. "Isn't that moss?"

Sydney checked it out. "It sure is," she confirmed. "That way is north."

She pointed in the direction that the mountain man went. "Let's hurry."

The girls squirmed around gangly bushes and past the branches of evergreen trees, and before long they saw bright sunlight not far ahead of them. The green grass surrounding the resort office came into view, and Sydney and Alexis hurried into the clearing.

"We got here before he did," said Sydney.

"I think it would be best if we were in the cabin," Alexis suggested. "That way, if he's watching, he won't know we were in the woods."

"Good idea," Sydney agreed.

They took off running, darting behind the resort office, staying away from the woods. They ran down a little hill to the back of their cabin. Sydney pulled the key out of her pocket and unlocked the door.

"Quick! Let's go to the front porch," said Alexis, rushing through the little kitchen and living room. She pushed open the front door and stepped onto the porch just in time to see Biscuit race out of the woods.

Ruff-ruff! Ruff-ruff! Ruff-ruff-aroof!

Alex opened the porch door and stepped outside to meet her furry friend.

"Biscuit, where have you been?" she said in a voice much louder than normal. "We've been worried sick about you!"

Sydney was close behind. "Why are you yelling?" she asked.

"I want that guy to hear me," said Alexis softly. "I want him to think that we were here all along."

Biscuit licked her hands.

Sydney looked toward the woods. The mountain man was nowhere in sight. "I think he's gone," she said.

Alexis held Biscuit at arm's length. "Oh, you smell *so* bad. We have to give you a bath. Why did you roll in that man's manure pile?"

"Manure pile!" Sydney shrieked.

"Didn't you hear him?" said Alexis. "He told Biscuit that he smelled bad, and then he said that Biscuit shouldn't have rolled in the manure pile."

"I must have missed that part," said Sydney, keeping her distance from Biscuit. "Manure is made up of animal droppings, like from cows and horses and sheep. Why in the world would he have a manure pile in the middle of a forest?"

Alexis picked Biscuit up and carried him onto the porch.

"Oh Alex, don't bring him in here," said Sydney. "He stinks."

"I know," her friend replied, "but if we don't keep him in the cabin, he might run away again. I'm not going back there. I'll get his leash and collar, and then we'll take him into the lake for a bath."

"I'll get them," said Sydney, walking toward the kitchen.

A few minutes later, Alexis buckled Biscuit's collar around his neck and hooked the leash onto the collar.

"Maybe the mountain man is keeping farm animals out there in the woods. Go get my shampoo from the bathroom, please," she told Sydney. "I'll meet you over by the dock."

Alexis opened the screen door and led Biscuit outside. He turned and pulled toward the woods. "No way, Biscuit!" she said. "You are *not* going back by that man. I wish you could talk, because I'd love to know what he's up to."

Sydney arrived with the shampoo. "Why would he have farm animals in the woods?" she asked. "It doesn't make any sense."

"Neither does the purple glow or the whispering woods," Alexis responded, kicking off her tennis shoes and wading into the water. "Come on, Biscuit." She held tight to his leash as the dog bounded into the lake splashing water all over her shorts.

"Okay, let's think about what we know," Sydney said as she opened the cap on the shampoo bottle. "We have a mountain man living in the forest. There's a spooky, purple glow in the woods, and something goes *whoosh* and talks. And a wolf, or whatever, belongs to the guy, and he has it tied up."

"Toss me the shampoo," said Alex. "And he has a manure pile. So that shovel probably belongs to him." She squeezed a generous amount of shampoo onto Biscuit's back. Then she tossed the bottle back to Sydney.

"And did you hear what he said about people finding out about him?" said Sydney. "He said if anyone found out what he was doing, it would be in the newspapers and on television. He's up to no good, Alex. I just know it."

"But he's kind to animals," her friend said. She was busy scrubbing Biscuit and had him so covered with lather that he looked like a little lamb. "Don't look now, but here comes that Duncan kid."

Duncan Lumley was heading for the dock carrying a fishing rod and tackle box. When he saw the girls washing the dog, he scowled. "What are you doing that for?" he said, walking right up to Sydney, almost getting in her face.

She took a step backward. "We're giving our dog a bath."

"Well, get him out of there," said Duncan. "You'll scare the fish away."

"Oh, for goodness sake," Sydney said. "You act like you own the place."

"I do," he said. "We come here every year."

Alexis rinsed Biscuit off and led him out of the water. He shivered, sending a shower of water all over Duncan.

"Hey!" Duncan cried, jumping backward. "Knock it off!"

"So what do you know about the guy who lives in the woods?" Sydney asked indifferently.

Alexis shot her a look. She couldn't believe that Sydney had asked Duncan such a thing.

The boy grinned. "I know all about him," he said. "He's the ghost of Jacques Chouteau."

Jacques Chouteau

"Who's Jock Show Toe?" Sydney asked.

Duncan smirked and shook his head. "Don't you know anything? It's a French name." Then, with a phony French accent, he said, *"Jacques Chouteau."*

Duncan's attitude irritated Sydney, but she tried to hold her temper. "Yeah, well, who is he?"

The redheaded boy walked onto the dock and opened his tackle box.

"I'm not telling," he said. He took a stubby, white Styrofoam container out of the box and opened the lid. He reached inside and pulled out a night crawler. "Catch." He flung it toward Sydney.

Sydney didn't flinch. The worm fell at her feet and quickly dug into the muddy soil.

"That's one less worm that you'll have for bait," Sydney announced. "Come on, Alexis, let's go."

"Yeah, you should go," Duncan told them. "I need to do some serious fishing."

Alexis walked ahead of Sydney, tightly holding Biscuit's

leash. He trotted a few steps forward and then stopped to shake the water off his soggy fur coat. When they were almost to the front porch, Biscuit decided to lie down and roll in the dirt.

"No, Biscuit!" Alexis said. She swept him into her arms and hurried through the door. "There," she said, setting him on a chair. "You behave yourself. You've gotten into enough trouble today."

Sydney stepped inside and closed the door. "We need to talk to Mrs. Miller in the office."

"What about?" Alexis asked.

"We need fishing poles. That brochure on the kitchen table says that the resort has some we can use. I also want to find out where to get bait."

"But we have dough balls," said Alexis, pointing toward the pizza dough thawing on the kitchen counter.

"I know," said Sydney. "But I think we each should fish with a different kind of bait. It'll give us a better chance at catching fish."

The girls shut Biscuit on the porch and headed up the driveway toward the office.

"Do you think Duncan told the truth about a ghost in the woods?" Alexis asked.

"I don't believe anything he says," said Sydney. "He was just trying to scare us. You didn't believe him, did you?"

Alexis kicked a stone to the side of the driveway. "I don't believe in ghosts," she said. "That guy in the woods is probably a very nice man—but I wish I knew that for sure."

Sydney opened the front door to the office, and the girls went inside.

Mrs. Miller wasn't at the desk. From somewhere inside the house came the sound of a soap opera on the television. Sydney rang the little metal bell next to a sign that read RING FOR SERVICE.

"Hey, look at this," said Alexis. She pointed to a painting on the wall. It showed a man dressed in a heavy fur coat with a big fur collar and a warm fur cap. In his left hand, he proudly held an animal skin. A caption at the bottom of the picture said JACQUES CHOUTEAU, FUR TRAPPER.

"Wow," said Sydney. "He really did exist."

Mrs. Miller pulled aside a curtain that hung in the doorway dividing the office from the living quarters. "Did you ring the bell?" she asked. She turned on the television behind the desk to her soap opera.

"I'm just wondering if we could get some fishing poles," said Sydney. "Alexis and I entered the contest."

A commercial interrupted the program, and Mrs. Miller turned her attention toward the girls. "Good for you!" she said. "Mr. Miller can certainly fix you up with some poles. Do you each have a fishing license?"

"No, ma'am," Sydney answered. "I didn't know that we needed one."

"You might," said Mrs. Miller. "My husband owns the bait shop. Go up to the road and turn right. In a little while you'll come to a restaurant called The Wave. The bait shop is next door. Charlie, that's my husband, will get you all fixed up." The commercial ended, and she turned back to the TV.

Sydney wanted to ask about the picture of Jacques Chouteau, but she could tell Mrs. Miller was too preoccupied with her program. "Thanks," she said as she and Alexis walked out the door. "See you later."

Charlie's Bait and Tackle was in a small, rundown building. It looked like an old garage set behind the parking lot of the restaurant, not far from the lakeshore. When the girls opened the front door, a strong, fishy smell filled their nostrils. They stood near a tank where hundreds of tiny gray fish darted to and fro. Fish trophies hung on the paneled walls. Around the trophies, the walls were lined with fishing poles and hundreds of fishing lures, spoons, and flies. An old paddle was propped in the corner behind the service counter. The words FISH TALES TOLD HERE were carved into it. A revolving rack on the counter held different kinds of fishing lines, and the front of the counter was a glass display case filled with various sizes of hooks.

"May I help you?" said a bald-headed man sitting behind the counter.

"The lady at the resort sent us," said Sydney.

"That would be my wife, Betty," the man said. "I'm Charlie."

Sydney walked over to the counter. "Mr. Miller, we need

59

a fishing license and some poles," she said. "And we'd like some bait, too, please."

The man smiled. "How old are you girls?"

"Twelve," said Sydney. "Almost thirteen."

"Kids under sixteen don't need a license," he said. "What kind of poles do you need?"

Alexis joined Sydney by the counter. "We're not sure. The brochure at the resort said that you have some poles that we can use," she said. "We're competing in the fishing contest."

"You are, are you?" said Mr. Miller. "Well, good for you. Usually, girls don't fish."

His comment irritated Sydney. *Why does everyone around here think that girls don't fish?* she thought.

"We're entering the dockside contest," she told him. "We're planning to catch the biggest fish."

"Well good. I hope you do," Mr. Miller said as he disappeared into a room next to the counter. He quickly returned with two fishing rods. "These are rods with reels," he said. "They're for the big fish."

Alexis took the pole and inspected it. "I've fished with cane poles," she said. "But I've never used one of these."

"I have," said Sydney. "But I'm not very good at it."

"Then come on outside, and I'll give you a lesson," Mr. Miller said.

It took a few tries for the girls to get comfortable using the rod and reel. Soon, they cast the line into the water

like pros. The reel allowed them to hang onto the pole
and throw the line a good distance into the water, way out
where the big fish swim.

Mr. Miller was friendly and helpful. He seemed
genuinely pleased that the girls had entered the contest.
He told them that they could use the poles for free, and he
gave them some bait—a small pail filled with water and two
dozen tiny gray fish called minnows. He also gave them a
Styrofoam container like the one Duncan had, filled with
squirming night crawlers.

Neither of the girls liked the idea of using live bait, but
Mr. Miller convinced them that they had to. "You can't
fish without live bait," he said. "If you want to be serious
contenders in the contest, then you have to get over being
squeamish."

Sydney had one more question before she and Alexis
left the bait shop. "What do you know about Jacques
Chouteau?" she asked.

"Oh, he's quite the legend around here," Mr. Miller said.
"Jacques Chouteau was a French fur trapper. He hung out
in northern Wisconsin way back in the 1800s. Mostly, he
trapped beavers around here. Then he skinned them and
sold their pelts to the Indians across the lake."

Mr. Miller took two ice-cream bars out of a nearby
freezer case and handed one to each of the girls. He opened
a can of soda for himself and sat down on a stool behind
the counter.

"They say Jacques made camp somewhere in the forest around here, though I don't know exactly where. There're caves deep in the woods, a bunch of 'em hidden under mounds of earth and among the trees, so you don't even know that they're there. Folks say old Jacques hid his furs inside those caves—and his money, too." Mr. Miller took a long drink of soda before he continued. "One day, he told folks he was gonna take his canoe over to the other side of the lake to do some trading at an Indian camp. That's the last anyone saw or heard from him. He set out across the lake on a nice, clear day, and he never came back."

Sydney licked the last bit of her vanilla ice cream off the wooden stick. "A kid at the resort says the ghost of Jacques Chouteau haunts the woods. Is that true?"

Mr. Miller put his elbows on the counter and leaned forward.

"Well, it just might be," he said mysteriously. "The legend says that Jacques Chouteau died in the woods, and his soul cries out sometimes. It moans, begging for someone to come and save him—"

Suddenly, the door swung open, and the girls jumped. The man from the lunch counter at the ice cream shop came inside. He had two buddies with him, and when he saw the girls with their fishing poles, he laughed.

"You girls are really serious about fishing in the contest, aren't you?" he said. "You haven't got a chance."

Sydney was about to give him a piece of her mind when

Mr. Miller came to her defense. "Now, Fred," he said. "Leave 'em alone. I think they'll do just fine."

The man named Fred walked past the girls like they were invisible. He took a spool of fishing line from the rack on the counter and paid for it. "My boy, Duncan, is gonna win the dock contest," he said. "He doesn't need these girls getting in his way."

Sydney felt her face turn hot. She was tempted to speak when Alexis tugged on her arm. "Let's go," she said. She thanked Mr. Miller for his help, and then they walked out the door.

"So that's Duncan's dad," Sydney said as they walked back to the resort. "It figures. They're both rude."

"We don't know them that well yet," said Alexis. "I'm sure there's something good about them. I don't think they're bad people. I remember on one TV show I watched, everyone hated this dad and son because they seemed obnoxious. But they turned out to be really nice."

Sydney said nothing.

It was almost suppertime, and when they got back to the cabin, Aunt Dee was on the porch reading a book. "Hey, girls," she said cheerfully. "How was your day?"

Biscuit slept near her feet looking like an angel.

"It was okay," Sydney told her. "We entered a fishing contest, and we just got back from the bait shop. Did you bring that list of fish that I texted you about?"

"It's on the kitchen table," Aunt Dee said. "And what's

that thawing on the counter?"

"Pizza dough," said Alexis. "We thought we'd make pizza for supper."

The girls got busy in the kitchen. They saved a glob of the dough for bait and put it in the refrigerator. Then Alexis rolled out the rest for the crust. Sydney sprinkled it with olive oil, spread on some tomato sauce, and put on the toppings. They made a salad, and before long the girls and Aunt Dee sat at the kitchen table eating delicious slices of gooey homemade pizza.

"This is so good, girls," said Aunt Dee. "I'm glad you thought of it. Since you made dinner, I'll take care of the dishes tonight."

Sydney popped the last bite of pizza into her mouth and drank some milk. "Thanks, Aunt Dee," she said. "We went to the ice cream shop this morning where they have a computer and free Internet. We set up a group chat with the Camp Club Girls for 6:30. We'd better get going."

"Be back before dark," Aunt Dee said.

"We'll leave Biscuit here," Alexis said. "He's not allowed inside the ice cream shop."

When they got to Tompkins' Ice Cream Shop, they found the tables and booths filled with customers enjoying after-dinner cones, malts, and sundaes. Sydney and Alexis walked to the back of the room and sat at the computer. They logged on to the Camp Club Girls private chat room where the other girls were waiting.

Sydney: *Looks like we're all here.*

Kate: *How's Biscuit?*

Sydney: *He's fine. How's Arizona?*

Kate: *Really hot, but fun.*

Bailey: *I told everyone about the mountain man.*

Sydney: *Well, here's an update. Biscuit ran into the woods today, and the mountain man got him.*

Kate: *NO WAY! Why did you let him off his leash? Is he all right?*

Alexis: *It's okay, Kate. He pulled out of his collar and ran into the woods, but he's fine. We went after him.*

Sydney: *We followed Biscuit into the forest. Then we saw this weird, purple glow, and heard a whooshing noise. It sounded like someone whispered, "Go back. Go back." So we ran and hid.*

McKenzie: *Wow, who do you think it was?*

Alexis: *We don't know. It didn't sound human. It sounded like trees were whispering.*

Bailey: *Trees don't whisper, Alex.*

Elizabeth: *Be careful. A forest can be dangerous.*

Alexis: *I know, but we had to get Biscuit. We hid and saw the mountain man carry Biscuit back to the cabin.*

Sydney: *We think he's up to no good. He told*

Biscuit if people found out about him, he'd be in the newspapers and on TV.

Elizabeth: *That man sounds creepy. Do you think he's a terrorist?*

Sydney: *He doesn't look like a terrorist, but neither did those guys we caught in Washington who planned to kill the President. We heard the ghost of an old fur trapper named Jacques Chouteau haunts the forest. Of course, we don't believe that. But we can't explain the purple light or the whispering. We need to investigate some more.*

Kate: *Be careful. The hotel we're at has overnight mail service. I'll send you some gadgets that might help you spy on him. Arizona is two hours behind Wisconsin, so I can send them today. You'll have them in the morning.*

Sydney: *Cool. We entered a fishing contest. Do you have any tips for catching big fish?*

McKenzie: *My brother always says be quiet, or you'll scare them. And you have to think like a fish and try to outsmart them.*

Bailey: *Dough balls for bait.*

Sydney: *We're making them tonight.*

Kate: *I'll send you my mini-microcamera and some other stuff. Maybe you can use some of it when you fish.*

Alexis: *Awesome!*

Elizabeth: *And I'll pray that God sends you tons of fish, just like He did when He fed the five thousand people in the Bible!*

Sydney: *I don't think we need five thousand fish, Beth. Just pray for us to catch the biggest one. We met this disgusting kid, Duncan, who acts like he's already won the contest. We're going to show him.*

Elizabeth: *Remember James 4:6 says that "God opposes the proud, but gives grace to the humble." Trust God to do what's best.*

Sydney: *Will do. Have to sign off now. Someone's waiting for the computer.*

A man and a little boy stood patiently near the workstation at the back of the shop. The boy was eating a chocolate ice cream cone, and it melted and dribbled down his arm.

Kate: *Please take very good care of Biscuit.*

Alexis: *I promise.*

Bailey: *Text me if anything happens, and I'll tell the girls.*

Sydney: *OK. Goodnight, everyone.*

As the girls walked away from the computer, Sydney's cell phone rang.

"Sydney?" Aunt Dee said. "I'd like you girls to come home. Mr. Miller just found a dead coyote on the beach. The man in Cabin Two saw something big run into the forest. He thinks it was a bear. I'd feel better if you were here."

Ghost Dog

When the girls got to the resort, Mr. Miller was walking toward the office. He carried a shovel, and his T-shirt was spattered with blood.

"Are you okay?" Sydney asked.

He wiped the sweat from his forehead. "I just buried a dead coyote. Something got him good. Nearly tore him apart."

Sydney's stomach churned. She loved animals. "What do you think did it?" she asked.

Mr. Miller set the shovel on the ground and wiped his hands on his overalls.

"I'm guessing a bear," he said. "I can't think of anything else that would tear an animal apart like that. Usually, a coyote can hold its own."

Alexis shuddered. "Do bears often kill things around here?"

"Not that much," said Mr. Miller. "When they do, it's mostly late at night, and they drag their prey into the woods to eat it. A bear coming at dusk and leaving what it killed isn't a good sign. It means it might be sick." He picked up the shovel. "You girls stay inside tonight, and keep your dog inside, too."

"Charlie, telephone!" Mrs. Miller stood on the front porch. She held a cordless phone.

Mr. Miller said, "If you need anything, call the office. Don't be out in the dark."

Alexis linked her arm in Sydney's as they walked to the cabin. "I just had a scary thought," she said.

"What about?" asked Sydney.

"Well, last week, I was playing a new Nancy Drew video game. It happens at a cabin on a lake. In it, a pack of howling ghost dogs attack her friend's house at night." Alexis took a deep breath. "Syd, you don't think—"

"Oh Alex, you don't believe the howling we heard in the woods was a ghost dog, do you?"

"I don't believe in ghosts," Alexis said. "But if I did, I'd think that the mountain man is the ghost of Jacques Chouteau, and Fang, his wolf or whatever that thing is, is a ghost, too. Of course, I don't believe that."

"So, we have to go back in the woods and find out what's really going on," said Sydney.

They were almost to the back door of the cabin. The sun had set behind the trees, and the sky was becoming dark. Whatever was in the woods was lurking in the darkness.

"We're not going into the woods tonight, Syd," said Alexis. "It's too dangerous with that bear, or whatever it is, hanging around." She opened the door to the cabin.

"I didn't mean tonight," said Sydney. "But tomorrow, maybe, in the bright daylight."

Biscuit ran to the back door to meet them. Alexis bent and patted him on the head. "What about the bear?" she asked.

"We'll need something to protect us," Sydney said.

"Protect you from what?" Aunt Dee's voice came from the living room.

"Careful," Sydney whispered. "Excellent hearing."

She closed the back door and flipped the lock.

The girls went into the living room where Aunt Dee sat on the floor playing the card game Solitaire.

"We were just talking about what would happen if we ran into the bear in the daylight tomorrow," said Sydney. "We were wondering how to protect ourselves."

"I've already thought of that," said Aunt Dee. "I'm going to give you some pepper spray to carry. It's a good idea for you to have protection in case you run into something, but only use it in a dire emergency. Understood? Only if your life depends on it."

"Understood," Sydney agreed.

"In the meantime, I called a ranger from the forest office. He's coming to look at the dead coyote. He should be able to tell what killed it." Aunt Dee uncovered the ace of spades and put it above the other cards on the floor.

"Good luck," said Sydney. "Mr. Miller already buried it."

"You're kidding!" Aunt Dee exclaimed. She put the two

of spades on top of the ace.

"Nope," Sydney said. "We met him on the driveway, and he told us all about it. He had a shovel in his hands, and his shirt was bloody."

Aunt Dee uncovered the king of hearts and laid it face up. "Well, maybe Ranger Geissman can find some evidence where the body was."

"Do we know for sure that a bear killed it?" Sydney asked.

"Mr. Miller said the man in Cabin Two saw something, but he couldn't say for sure what it was," said Aunt Dee. "He said that it was big, and it moved very fast."

Sydney took the leftover dough out of the refrigerator. "Cabin Two is the Lumleys.'"

"How do you know that?" asked her aunt.

"We've seen the kid, Duncan, a couple of times. He's rude. So is his dad. He thinks it's really dumb that Alex and I entered the fishing contest."

Sydney opened a can of tuna, and Biscuit came running into the kitchen to investigate the smell. "He told Mr. Miller that he doesn't want a couple of girls getting in the way of Duncan winning the contest."

Sydney mixed the tuna with the dough and rolled it into little balls. Then she rolled them in cornmeal.

Soon, the beams from a car's headlights flashed through the cabin windows. Sydney looked outside and saw a Park Service car pull up to their back door. "I think the ranger's here," she said.

The girls and Aunt Dee went out to meet him.

"So, where's the dead coyote?" Ranger Geissman asked.

"The resort owner buried it," said Aunt Dee. "But maybe we can find enough evidence to get some idea about what killed it."

She got her flashlight from the kitchen table, and they all walked to the shore. "It was right over here," said Aunt Dee.

Ranger Geissman shined his flashlight on the sandy strip at the edge of the lake. The only pieces of evidence left were a few spots of blood and gobs of matted, gray fur. "Well," he said, "looks like there was a struggle here. Looks like the coyote tried to fight off whatever got it. Usually, a coyote won't get much of a chance to fight with a bear. A bear attacks, and that's it."

He walked around the area looking for clues. "This is interesting," he said. "Looks like two sets of canine footprints here. Charlie Miller found just one body, right?"

Aunt Dee shined her flashlight on the ground to get a better look at the prints. "That's right. Just one dead coyote, and the man in Cabin Two saw something run away."

"Did he say what it was?" asked Ranger Geissman.

"He thought it was a bear, but he wasn't sure. He just said it was big and fast."

AR-AR-AR-ROoooooooooooooooooooooo. . .AR-AR-AR-ROoooooooooooooooooooooo. . . A mournful cry came from deep in the forest. Sydney whispered in Alexis's ear. "It's Fang!"

"Well, there's your answer," said the ranger. "I think a

big wolf killed your coyote. If you look at this other set of prints, you can see they're huge. They're not coyote, but definitely canine and probably a wolf."

He walked up and down the narrow beach looking for more evidence. "I don't see any sign of a bear," he said. "And no blood trail leading into the woods, so the other dog must not have been badly injured. Looks like a dog fight to me. Most likely your coyote tangled with a good-sized wolf."

Aunt Dee sighed with relief.

"Well, that's good to hear," she said. "The last thing we need is a sick bear wandering around. Will you stop at the office and tell the Millers what you found?"

"Will do," said Ranger Geissman, walking to his car. "And I hope you get the job at the ranger station," he added. "You'd be good on our team."

"Thanks," said Aunt Dee. "I hope so, too."

The ranger drove to the office, and Aunt Dee and the girls went back inside.

Boom! Boom! Boom!

Someone pounded hard on the front door.

Boom! Boom! Boom!

"Now who would that be?" Aunt Dee wondered. She walked to the door and peeked through the curtains on the window. "It's Mr. Lumley from Cabin Two." Aunt Dee opened the door. Fred Lumley stood there with Duncan at his side.

"We want to know what's going on over here," Mr. Lumley said.

Aunt Dee invited them in. "Why, nothing's going on," she said. "What do you mean?"

Mr. Lumley looked around the cabin as if he expected someone to be there. Meanwhile, Duncan stood next to him with a snide grin on his face.

"Dunk here, said you were all wandering by the lake with flashlights. Then he saw a police car drive away. If there's trouble, I want to know."

Aunt Dee got her backpack from the bedroom and unzipped it. She took out her ranger identification badge and handed it to Duncan's dad. "I'm Dee Powers," she said. "I'm a US Park Ranger. Another ranger and I were trying to find out what killed the coyote on the beach."

Duncan's face lit up. "You're a park ranger!" he said. "No way."

"Way!" said Aunt Dee, smiling.

"But ladies can't be park rangers—can they, Dad?"

Duncan's father looked at the ID and smirked. "Looks like they can, Dunk," he said, handing the ID back to Aunt Dee. "So what did the other ranger think happened to the coyote? I told the Millers that I saw something big hurry into the woods. I'm sure it was a bear."

"You're sure it was a bear, or you *think* it was a bear?" said Aunt Dee.

Mr. Lumley ignored her question. "So what did the guy ranger say?"

Duncan stood with his hands on his hips. Once in a

while, he glanced toward the kitchen at the cookie sheet filled with dough balls.

The smile disappeared from Aunt Dee's face. Sydney could tell she was as irritated with Fred Lumley as Sydney was with Duncan.

"Nothing proved it was a bear attack," said Aunt Dee. "We saw another set of tracks on the beach, probably a wolf's. Ranger Geissman and I agreed that the coyote's death was the result of a dog fight. So Mr. Lumley, you and Duncan have nothing to worry about. There's no bear, and everything is under control."

"Come on, Dunk," said Mr. Lumley, putting his hand on his son's shoulder. "Let's go." They turned and walked out the door. As they did Fred Lumley mumbled, "I know what I saw."

"Have a nice evening," Aunt Dee replied cheerfully.

Neither Mr. Lumley nor Duncan answered.

"Well, those are a couple of happy fellows, aren't they?" said Sydney's aunt, shutting the door.

"You haven't seen the worst of them," Sydney told her. "Duncan is a real pain, but I'm going to show him. Tomorrow, when Alex and I start fishing, he'll wish that he'd never come to North Twin Lake."

She went to the kitchen and loaded the dough balls into a plastic bag. "I've got a secret weapon. While Alex fishes with live bait, I'll be fishing with these—some nice, tasty tuna treats for the big guys."

"Well then, you'd better turn in early," Aunt Dee said. "The fish bite best at dawn."

Sydney and Alexis went to their room to study the fish booklet that Aunt Dee had brought from the ranger station. They needed to research which fish were the biggest and how to catch them.

"Muskies," said Sydney.

"Huh?" Alexis wondered.

"We need to fish for muskies. *Esox masquinongy* is the scientific name. Also known as muskellunge, lunge, maskinonge, and great pike. The Ojibwa Indians called them *maashkinoozhe*, which means ugly fish. It says here that you catch them by casting, and they like spoon lures or live bait."

"What's a spoon lure?" asked Alexis. She took some hand lotion from her bag, put a glob in the palm of her hand, and offered some to Sydney.

"I'm not sure exactly," Sydney said, squeezing lotion onto her hands. "The bait shop probably has them, but I think we should just stick to our live bait and the dough balls. It says that the world record for the biggest muskie is almost 70 pounds."

"Oh Syd! How will we handle a 70-pound fish? We don't weigh much more than that." Alexis sat down on Sydney's bed.

Sydney continued reading. "The average size for a big muskie in North Twin Lake is 35 to 40 inches. It doesn't say how much a fish that size weighs. The rules for the fishing contest say that the fish are measured by length, not weight. Here's a picture." She handed the booklet to Alexis.

"Oh, it's ugly!" Alexis exclaimed. "But it can't help the way it looks. Poor fish."

The picture showed a long, silver brown fish. It had brown stripes on its body and spots on its tail. The eyes were glaring and the nose was short. Its lower jaw stuck out in a long underbite.

"It has teeth!" said Alexis.

"Yeah, I know," Sydney said. "Look at the caption under the picture. It says the teeth are as sharp as surgical scalpels, and you should never stick your hand into its mouth."

"As if I would want to stick my hand in there," said Alexis. "I'm sure we'll be fine. But Sydney, do you really want to do this?"

"I do!" said Sydney. "We're going to show Duncan Lumley how to fish. Tomorrow we'll catch the biggest muskie in North Twin Lake."

"Well then," Alexis said, standing. "We'd better get ready for bed and get a good night's sleep. We have to be up before dawn."

She headed for the bathroom holding her toothbrush and pajamas. "And if we catch one of those things, you're going to take it off the hook."

Before long, the girls turned off the light in their room,

said their prayers, and settled into their beds. Sydney rolled over and faced the window. She opened it a few inches to let in some fresh air.

"Hey," she said. "I can see that purple glow."

Alexis climbed down from her bunk and looked. "Oh yeah," she said. "The tops of the trees are glowing lavender. Is that spooky or what?"

Sydney sat up in her bed and made room for Alexis. The two of them gazed out the window at the purple light.

"What do you think causes it?" Alexis asked. "It's pretty in a strange way."

Sydney put the window up a little more. "I can't think of anything in a forest that lights up," she said. "When Bailey came to visit me at my grandparents' house at the ocean, we saw the waves glowing at night. It was something called *bioluminescence*. Billions of living organisms in the water glowing from a chemical reaction. It was really pretty. Everything glowed sort of green and blue."

Alexis put her face nearer the window screen. "So do you think maybe some sort of giant organism is out there in the forest that's causing it to glow purple?" she asked.

"You mean like a giant glowworm, or a monster mutant firefly?" Sydney grinned.

"Very funny," said Alexis. "But what if billions of tiny organisms live deep in the forest, and they glow purple? That's a possibility, isn't it?"

"I suppose," said Sydney.

79

Suddenly, Alexis gasped. "Did you see that?"

Sydney did see. Something big was out there again lurking near the picnic table. It was in the shadows, just like the night before. And this time, the girls were certain that it was the mountain man. The moon was bright enough for them to see his form. He walked about slowly with a long stick, picking at the earth."

"What's he doing?" Sydney whispered.

"I'm not sure," said Alexis. "I think he's digging in the dirt." She moved over so Sydney could get a better look.

"He has some sort of bag," Sydney said. "It looks like he's collecting things. He is! I just saw him pick something up and put it in the bag. What do you think?"

"I think you're right," said Alexis. "*Shhhh!* Listen."

From just beneath the window, came a soft, rhythmic panting sound. Someone, or something, was breathing hard like it had just run a race, and then—

"Oh!" Sydney cried, slamming down the window. Looking in at them was the head of a huge, black dog. Its eyes glowed, and its open mouth was filled with sharp menacing teeth.

Girls Can Fish

The sun was just peeking over the horizon when Sydney and Alexis went out to fish. Neither girl had slept much the night before. The dog's head had scared them both. It disappeared so quickly when Sydney shut the window that she wondered if they had only imagined its wild eyes and spiky teeth.

No. She was sure of it. The mountain man and his dog were real.

Sydney carried her fishing rod and the bag of dough balls onto the dock. Alexis followed with her pole and a small pail filled with minnows.

"You dropped a dough ball," Alexis said. She bent over to pick it up. "Hey, this isn't a dough ball. It's a big mushroom!"

Sydney set her fishing pole on the end of the dock. She looked at the brown mushroom, about as big as a ping-pong ball, in the palm of Alexis's hand. "That's weird," she said.

"Look, I see more floating in the water," said Alexis.

A dozen mushroom caps floated in the water beside the dock.

"Someone must have made a salad or something and tossed them away," Sydney said. She took the mushroom from Alexis's hand and threw it as far as she could into the lake. The mushroom barely landed on the water's surface when a big fish leaped up into the air. It made a narrow arch and plunged back into the lake with a splash, taking the mushroom with it.

"Wow, did you see that?" Sydney asked.

"I think it was a muskie," said Alexis.

The girls sat on the dock and got their fishing lines ready.

"I hate this," Alexis said, sticking the hook into one of the minnows. "I feel like a murderer. I don't know why I let you talk me into using the live bait."

Sydney was busy loading a dough ball onto the end of her line. At first, the dough didn't stay on the hook, but after a while she figured out how to squish it just right so it stuck.

"Don't look now, but here comes trouble," said Alexis.

Duncan Lumley and his dad walked toward the dock. Sydney and Alexis cast their lines into the lake and pretended not to see.

"Get out of my spot," Duncan said.

"I didn't see your name on it," Sydney replied.

"I always fish here," said Duncan.

Mr. Lumley stood by his son. A toothpick dangled from his mouth. He wore a life jacket and carried a fishing rod and tackle box. "This is where Dunk fishes," he said.

Sydney refused to look at him. "Each cabin has a dock, and this one is ours. Duncan can fish on his own dock."

From the corner of her eye, she saw Duncan step forward. His dad grabbed him by the arm and stopped him.

"They're girls, Dunk," he said. "They don't know any better. Come on. You can fish with me in the boat."

"If I fish from the boat, I can't enter what I catch in the contest," Duncan complained. "And I wanna win!"

"Well then," his dad said, "I suppose you'll have to fish from *our* dock." He gave the girls a dirty look, and then he walked away.

Sydney turned and smiled at Duncan. His green eyes flashed, and he stormed off stomping his feet.

"Don't you bother my boy while he's fishing," Mr. Lumley called to them over his shoulder. "Cast away from his line, and don't get in his space."

"Will do," Sydney said.

Mr. Lumley stepped onto the dock by Cabin Two. As the girls watched, he untied the aluminum boat from the dock. He pulled the cord on the outboard motor and revved it. Then he steered the boat into the lake, speeding past Dock One, nearly clipping the lines from Sydney's and Alexis's poles.

"Ooooo, he's just as irritating as Duncan!" said Sydney. She reeled in her line and cast it again, trying another spot farther out. At the same time Duncan stood at the end of his dock and cast his line into the water.

"Hang in there, Syd," said Alexis. "Remember what the

Bible says: 'Losing self-control leaves you as helpless as a city without a wall.' That's Proverbs 25:28."

"You've gotten almost as good as Beth at quoting scripture," said Sydney.

Alexis reeled in her line a little bit. "I'm trying to learn a verse a day.

"Hey, I think I've got something!" The tip of her pole bent down toward the water.

"Reel it in, Alex! Reel it in!" Sydney cried.

Alexis leaned back and pulled against the tension on her line. She turned the crank on the reel hard and fast.

"Go, Alex! Go!" Sydney shouted. "Don't look now, but Duncan has something, too."

Duncan stood on Dock Two reeling in his fish just as hard and as fast as Alexis. Then, all of a sudden, he yelled. "Stop! Hey! Stop reeling in your line!"

Alexis glanced over at him. "I think he's yelling at me," she said.

Duncan was jumping up and down. "Stop reeling!" he shouted. "You're tangled in my line!"

But it was too late. The fishing pole flew out of Duncan's hands and splashed into the water. As Alexis turned the crank on her reel, she watched his pole moving nearer to her dock.

"Oh, oh," said Sydney. "Here he comes."

Duncan rushed onto the dock where the girls were fishing. He took the pole out of Alexis's hands and reeled in her line. When he reached down to pick his pole out of the water, Sydney felt like pushing him in.

"This is why girls shouldn't fish," Duncan said, untangling his line from Alexis's.

"*Listen,*" Sydney said, raising her voice a little. "We were here fishing first. You knew where we'd cast our lines, and you *deliberately* threw yours near ours. So don't blame *us* for the trouble."

She stood and faced Duncan. He stepped back. She realized she was at least a head taller than he was, and she had muscles—Sydney kept in shape. Duncan, on the other hand, didn't look at all strong.

"Let's just try to get along," she said, lowering her voice. "Okay?"

Duncan backed off. "Okay," he said, nearly whispering. He freed the last bit of his line and reeled it onto his pole.

"Hey, what's this stuff?" He pointed to the bag of dough balls.

"Bait," said Sydney. She picked up the bag and held it protectively.

"What kind of bait?" asked Duncan.

"Secret bait," Sydney said.

"Yeah, well, it's not as good as mine," Duncan told her. "Hey, did you hear that howling last night?"

Alexis put another minnow on her hook. She asked Sydney and Duncan to stand back, and with all her might, she cast her line into the lake. "We heard it," she said.

"What do you think it was?"

"The ghost of Jacques Chouteau," Duncan said matter-of-factly.

"What makes you think so?" Sydney asked. She picked up her pole from the dock and continued fishing.

"Everyone knows the story," said Duncan. "Old Jacques got trapped in a cave in the forest. An avalanche or something trapped him inside, and he died in there. Now, his ghost howls to get out. *Ow-wooooooo....* And sometimes he says, 'I'm gonna get you. I'm gonna get you. I'm gonna get you!'" Duncan put his arms in the air and walked like a monster toward the girls.

"Just ignore him," Sydney said.

"I am," Alexis agreed.

"Aw, come on." Duncan sighed, putting his hands on his hips. "Don't you have a sense of humor?"

"You're not funny," said Sydney.

Then something pulled hard on her line. She held tight to the pole with both hands and yanked. All at once, the crank on her reel spun around and around making the line shoot forward.

"Hang on! You got something," Duncan cried. "Here, let me do it." He reached for Sydney's pole.

"Get away!" Sydney said, shoving him with one shoulder.

"Aw, come on," said Duncan. "You got something big on there. Let me reel it in. You don't know what you're doing."

"No!" said Sydney.

Alexis thrust her pole into Duncan's hands. "Here," she said. "Hold this." Then she grabbed the handle of Sydney's pole with both hands and helped her to hang on. "Reel it in, Syd," she said.

"Nice and slow," Duncan added.

Sydney let the fish take a little more line. Then she reeled it in. She did it again and again. Suddenly, she felt a strong jerk on the line. Then the fish shot up and out of the water! It was about twenty yards offshore, and when it splashed back into the lake, it fought hard against the hook.

"Oh man, you got a muskie on there," said Duncan.

Sydney couldn't tell if he was excited or complaining. She fought the fish until it was too tired to fight. Then she reeled it in. "Here it comes," she said. "Here it comes."

The fish's long snout appeared near the dock. The muskie opened and closed its mouth and thrashed in the water.

"It's huge!" Alexis squealed.

The fish was way too heavy for Sydney to lift by herself, besides she was afraid of its teeth. "Now what?" she asked.

"I dunno," said Alexis. She looked at Duncan.

"You gotta get it in your net," he said. Then he looked around the dock. "Don't tell me you don't have a net."

Sydney hadn't even considered that they might need one. She should have known that they would need help lifting a big fish up onto the dock.

Alexis sensed Sydney's embarrassment.

"We can do it," she said. "Come on, Syd. We can both

grab it and lift it up." Alexis got down on all fours and leaned over the edge of the dock.

"No," said Duncan. "Wait." He turned and sprinted toward Dock Two. Soon he was back with his net. "Here, I'll help you."

"Thanks, but no thanks," said Sydney. Secretly, she wished she hadn't said it. She needed that net, but she didn't trust Duncan to help her.

"Aw, come on," Duncan said. "I'm not going to do anything. Besides, I can tell already that it's not a winning fish."

He pushed between the girls and scooped the fish into his net.

Sydney saw that he struggled to lift it up. She reached over and grabbed onto the handle, and together they pulled the net onto the dock. "Remember," she said. "Helping me to net it doesn't give you any rights to the fish."

"I don't want your dumb old fish," said Duncan. Carefully, he removed the hook from the fish's mouth. Then he took a small tape measure from his pocket and measured it as it lay gasping on the dock.

"Thirty-two and a half inches," he said. "Not big enough."

"How do you know?" Alexis asked.

Duncan took his cell phone out of his back pocket. He punched in some numbers. "Didn't you read the rules?" he said. "When you catch a fish, you call Tompkins' and text FISH. They'll send you a message saying what the biggest catch is so far. If it's less than that, you've gotta let the fish go."

"I don't believe you," said Sydney.

Duncan's cell phone rang. "Look," he said, handing her the phone. "The message on the screen says 34 INCHES. See? Not big enough."

Sydney looked at the muskie flopping on the dock.

"He's right, Syd," said Alexis. "I read the rules again this morning. If it's not the biggest fish, you're supposed to release it."

She reached down and grasped the fish around its middle, steering clear of the razor-sharp teeth in its huge, gaping mouth. The fish's body was motionless; it seemed to melt in her hands. With all her might, Alexis pushed it off the dock and into the water.

"Swim away," she said. "Go on. Swim."

The big fish treaded water just below the surface. Then, sensing that it was free, it shot away from the dock.

"Wow," said Duncan. "You touched it and everything."

"Yeah," said Alexis. "So what?"

"So, girls don't touch fish," Duncan said. But this time his voice sounded confused.

Sydney sighed deeply.

"Listen," she said. "I've had it with all this *girls don't* stuff. Girls do a lot of things that boys do. If your mom wanted to, *she* could fish. So could your sister. And if they wanted to, they could touch the fish and *everything*!"

"I don't have a mom, and I don't have a sister," said Duncan. "It's just me and my dad."

Suddenly, Duncan seemed different and not so much of a bully.

"Well, anyhow," Sydney said softly, "thanks for your help."

Duncan picked up his net. "Not a problem. And don't forget, I'm going to win the contest."

He started walking toward the end of the dock. "And don't get your line anywhere near mine." He looked over his shoulder at Alexis. "Next time, I won't be so understanding."

He went back to Dock Two, baited his hook, and cast his line into the water.

"I can't figure that kid out," said Sydney. "For a minute there, I thought maybe he wanted to be our friend."

Alexis threw her line back into the lake. "He is a bit strange. And what did you make of what he said about Jacques Chouteau's ghost? Do you think he was really trapped in a cave and died there?"

Sydney put another dough ball on her hook and cast her line. "It all adds up with what Mr. Miller said. Remember? He said Jacques hid his money and furs in a cave and that he died in the woods."

"But he didn't say anything about him dying in a cave," said Alexis.

"No," Sydney said. "The legend says that he died in the woods, and he haunts them."

Alexis was quiet for a while. "Well, I don't believe it, do you?"

"Do I believe that he's a ghost? No," said Sydney. "But we know that Jacques Chouteau was a real person, so it's possible he might have died in a cave in the woods. Something is out there. And it lurks in a spooky, purple light, and it hangs around with some sort of big dog that howls and maybe kills coyotes."

"Oh Syd," said Alexis, easing her grip on the pole. "Do you think that thing we saw last night killed the coyote? It sure didn't look like a wolf."

Sydney turned the crank on her reel and added some slack to her line. "I'm sure it wasn't a wolf," she said. "It was much bigger than a wolf, and black, and not at all shaggy. And Alexis, when that thing stood up, it must have been six feet tall!"

"I know," said Alexis. "I don't even want to think about it. I couldn't believe my eyes."

"Neither could I," said Sydney. "In fact, when I woke up this morning, I wondered if it had all been a dream—just something in my imagination."

Alexis reeled in her line a bit. "It wasn't your imagination, Sydney. I saw it, too. I think it was his dog—*Fang.*"

They fished silently for a while. The sun was up over the trees now, and its reflection on the water hurt their eyes. Alexis watched Sydney's pole while Sydney went back to the cabin and got their sunglasses.

"You know," Sydney said when she returned. "I just

91

saw that mushroom book on your nightstand, the one you found on the ground yesterday morning."

"Yeah, what about it?" Alexis said lazily.

"Well," Sydney continued, "it's a field guide to mushrooms. And we just found a mushroom on the dock and more floating in the water. Do you think they're somehow connected?"

"They could be," said Alexis. "What are you thinking?"

"I don't know yet what I'm thinking," said Sydney. "But maybe they have something to do with the mountain man."

"Could be," said Alexis. "Maybe he's a farmer or something."

"No," said Sydney. "My instinct tells me that he's not a farmer. I don't know yet what he is, but we're going to find out. And when we do, we'll know what that purple light is, too, and the howling."

"*Whoo-hooo!*"

A shout came from Dock Two. Duncan stood, pole in hand, fighting with something on the end of his line. As the girls watched, he reeled it in. He dunked his net into the water and, after almost falling in, he scooped a big fish onto the dock.

Duncan took out his tape measure.

"Thirty-five and a half inches!" he shouted.

CHAPTER
8

Into the Woods

Kate's package arrived as promised.

"Great," said Sydney. "Let's see what's in here." She put the box on the kitchen table and got a sharp knife from the drawer. Carefully, she cut the tape that held the box shut.

"Hurry," said Alexis. "I want to see what Inspector Gadget sent us."

The lid popped open. The first thing Sydney saw was a watch.

"Cool!" she said. "Kate sent us the Wonder Watch."

Kate loved inventing things, and the Wonder Watch was one of her best creations. It could connect to a computer, surf the net, and read e-mail. Kate set it up so that with the push of a button, the girls would be connected to the Camp Club Girls chat room.

Also in the box was a plastic bag, carefully wrapped and surrounded by Styrofoam peanuts. Sydney removed the wrapping and pulled out a pair of mirrored sunglasses.

"Check this out," she said. "Kate gave us a note. 'If you wear these, you can see what's behind you.' "

She handed the glasses to Alexis.

"Whoa," Alex said after she put them on. "This is weird. Depending on where I look through the lenses, I can see straight ahead or behind me. These are awesome, but they'll take getting used to. Here. You try them."

Sydney put the glasses on and looked in front of her. "Oh!" She gasped.

"What?"

"I saw someone looking in the window behind me." Just then, there came a soft knock on the back door. The girls saw Mr. Miller standing on the little concrete porch. "Hi, Mr. Miller," Sydney said, opening the door.

"Howdy," he said. "Nice sunglasses. Say, I hear that you might need one of these." He held up a fishing net. "And one of these, too." He handed Sydney a metal tape measure. "So, you caught a big one this morning, huh?"

"You must have been talking to Duncan," said Alexis.

Mr. Miller took off his baseball cap and scratched his head. "Well, let's just say that a little bird told me."

He gave Sydney the net, and she put it on the table next to Kate's box.

"Well, that little bird has been giving us plenty of trouble since we got here," Sydney said. "And his dad hasn't been very nice, either."

Mr. Miller plopped his cap back on his head. "Well, that's kinda what I wanted to talk to you about. You see, Duncan's not a bad kid. His family's been comin' here since he was a baby. Then a couple of years ago, his mom and sister were killed in a car accident. Duncan and his dad haven't been the same since. His dad's still mad that it happened, and poor Duncan gets the worst of it sometimes. I don't think he has many friends."

A guilty feeling sank into the pit of Sydney's stomach. "I'm glad you told us," she said.

"Me, too," Alexis added. "We'll pray for them."

Mr. Miller smiled. "You seem like nice girls. I figured you'd give Duncan a break and try to be friends with him."

"We'll try," said Sydney. "And thanks for the net and the tape measure."

"You're welcome," he said. "Good luck with your fishing, and may the best man. . .er. . .I mean. . .um. . .may the best man or woman win!"

He tipped the brim of his cap and walked back toward the office.

Sydney closed the door. "Well, that might explain why Duncan is so mean," she said. "I can't imagine how I'd feel if my mom and brother died."

"Me neither," said Alexis. "We'll add Duncan and his dad to our prayers every night. And Syd, let's be nice to Duncan—as hard as that might be."

There were three more things in Kate's box. One was a GPS locator.

"Great!" Sydney said. "Now we won't have to worry about making trails in the woods and getting lost."

The second item was a tiny camera, about the size of a matchbox. Kate had included another note:

This is a mini-microcamera with a hand-held monitor. It takes pictures and videos. You can set it up like a security camera and watch the monitor to see what's going on. You can also use it under water. I programmed it so every picture you take will automatically show up on our web site.

Sydney unpacked the monitor, which was about the size of a cell phone.

"This is so cool," she said. "So do you want to do some exploring?"

"You mean sleuthing?" Alexis asked.

"That's exactly what I mean," said Sydney. "Let's go into the woods and find out what that mountain man is up to."

Sydney loaded the gadgets inside her waist pack and strapped it around her middle. In the meantime, Alexis slipped the Wonder Watch over her wrist. She took her cell phone out of her pocket and flipped it open.

"I'm texting Kate to let her know that we got the package. Then I'll text the other girls and tell them that we're going into the woods. Maybe some of them will be online if we need them."

"Good idea," said Sydney.

"And Syd, don't forget the pepper spray in case we run

into a bear," Alexis reminded her.

"I got it," said Sydney.

The girls entered the forest following the same route they'd taken the day before. After they'd walked about ten minutes, they noticed the shovel on the ground.

"Hey look," said Sydney. "Someone's been digging again."

The earth near the shovel was freshly turned over, and the tip of the shovel was caked with mud.

"Do you think that's where Mr. Miller buried the coyote?" Alexis asked.

"I don't think so," said Sydney. "We're too far from the resort. And look at how the ground is dug up. Whoever dug here didn't dig one big hole. The person dug a bunch of little ones."

Alexis gave the earth a closer look. "It looks like clumps are missing out of the soil."

Sydney picked up the shovel.

"What are you doing?" Alexis asked.

"I'm going to dig and see what's here," Sydney said. "Maybe I'll find the lost treasure of Jacques Chouteau." She grinned.

"Don't," said Alexis. "At least not now. Whoever dug here will probably come back. We'd better not mess things up. Otherwise, whoever it is will know for sure that we're watching them."

"You're right," said Sydney. She put the shovel back on the ground, careful to place it exactly as she'd found it.

"What are those things over there?" Alexis asked. She pointed to a brownish white mass on the forest floor a few yards away.

"Mushrooms!" said Sydney. "Gigandimundo mushrooms."

She took a closer look and snapped a picture with the mini-microcam. "I don't know what kind they are, but there's a ton of them all over the place. I didn't notice them when we were here before."

"Neither did I," said Alexis.

Dozens of mushrooms popped out of the rotted leaves and pine needles on the forest floor. Their umbrella-shaped caps were rough and bumpy like the wool on a sheep, and their edges were ragged. The black-and-white caps sat atop thick little trunks that were scaly and peeling.

"Do you think they're edible?" Alexis wondered.

"I don't know," said Sydney. "Some mushrooms you can eat, but others are poisonous. I think we should leave them alone. Definitely, though, we need to check out this spot and find out who's digging here."

"Maybe it's one of the visitors at the resort," said Alex. "These things are probably edible, and someone is digging them up for cooking."

The girls walked farther into the woods searching for clues as they went. After a while, they found a narrow path going east and decided to follow it.

"I think we're walking toward the lake," said Alexis. "I hear a motorboat."

"Me, too," said Sydney. "A bunch of boats were on the lake when we left. Shhhh! Listen."

Alexis heard it, too. Someone whistled a quick and lively tune. It came from the south—in the woods—and with each happy note it got closer.

"Hide!" said Alexis. "Over there in those bushes."

The girls scrambled behind a thick cluster of honeysuckle. They stood silently watching the path through the dense leaves. Sydney took the mirrored sunglasses out of her waist pack and put them on.

"I don't want anyone sneaking up on us," she whispered.

The whistling stopped. The girls heard a rustling. Something was trying to force its way through the brush on the other side of the path. Twigs snapped, and the tops of small saplings swayed.

"Doggone it!" a man grumbled. More twigs snapped. The brush on the other side of the path trembled. "Come on. . . . *Ugh! Ooof! Umph!*"

Suddenly, a bright orange object thrust through the bushes and fell onto the path. It was nine feet long, and it looked like a giant kazoo. The middle part was hollowed out to form a little place with a seat. A long pole was strapped to the side of the thing with a rounded paddle on either end.

"It's a kayak." Sydney whispered so softly that Alexis could barely hear.

A heavy brown boot emerged from the thicket, then

a leg wearing worn khaki pants, a thick brown belt, a red plaid shirt, an arm, a hand. Finally, the mountain man pushed through the brush and onto the path. His cap had come off, and he held it in one hand. Burrs and brambles covered his shaggy beard and hair.

"Dad burn it!" he complained. "There has to be a better way through the woods to this path."

He picked up his cap and plopped it onto his head. "Ow!"

He took it off again and picked the brambles out of his hair. While the girls watched, he tilted the kayak onto its edge with the bottom facing him. He gripped the center rim, hoisted the boat onto his upper leg, and then wrestled it onto his shoulder. "There," he puffed. Then off he went down the path, whistling his happy song.

"Let's follow him," whispered Alexis. "Are you going to take off those glasses?"

"I think I'll leave them on," said Sydney. "In case Fang is nearby."

They followed a safe distance behind as the mountain man slogged along toward the shore.

"Wait!" said Alexis.

"What's the matter?" Sydney asked.

"The Wonder Watch is doing something. I feel it jiggling on my wrist." Alexis looked at the face of the watch. Words flashed across the screen. MESSAGE WAITING: BAILEY. "What do I do?" she asked.

"Push the button on the side," Sydney said.

Alexis pushed the button, and Bailey's message scrolled across the watch's big, round face. WHAT'S WITH THE UGLY 'SHROOM? HAVE YOU GUYS SEEN THE OLD MAN IN THE WOODS YET?

"Can I text back on this thing?" Alex asked.

"No, but you can talk back," said Sydney. "Just say what you want, and a microchip inside will translate it into printed words. They'll show up in the chat room."

"I forgot all the extra stuff that Kate built into this thing," said Alex. "I've never used it."

She put her lips up to the face of the watch and spoke softly. "They're growing all over the place in the forest. We don't know what kind they are. We're following the mountain man now. More later."

"Come on. Let's go," said Sydney. "He's probably to the lake already."

By the time they got to the lakeshore, the mountain man had already launched his kayak. They could see him paddling swiftly across the lake, heading directly to the other side.

Sydney searched the muddy earth for clues. "Hey, I think these are his boot prints," she said. "A word is on the bottom of the soles."

She took out the mini-microcam and took a picture. "I can't read it very well, but maybe the Camp Club Girls can enlarge it and tell us what it says. Send a message on the Wonder Watch. Ask them to blow up the picture."

While Sydney and Alexis waited for the girls to reply, the mountain man steered his kayak to the other side of the lake. He pulled it up onto the shore and disappeared into the forest.

"The watch is jiggling again," said Alexis. "It's a message from Elizabeth." She held out her wrist and pushed the button so Sydney could see.

I ENLARGED THE PHOTO. THE WORD ON THE SOLE IS *ÉSPRIT*. I TOOK FRENCH LAST SEMESTER. IT MEANS SPIRIT.

Sydney felt a chill. "This is spooky, Alex," she said. "I mean, think about the legend of Jacques Chouteau. He paddled off across North Twin Lake and was never heard from again. He was French. Now, we find this French word on the bottom of this boot print, and it means 'spirit.' It's too weird."

"You know what's weird?" Alex said. "Seeing my reflection in those mirrored sunglasses!"

"Sorry," said Sydney. She took off the glasses and put them in her pack.

"Syd, you don't really believe that he's the ghost of Jacques Chouteau, do you?"

Sydney hesitated. "No," she said. "But you have to admit it's strange." She started walking up the narrow path and into the woods.

Alexis followed her. "Where are we going now?"

"We're going to find the purple glow," said Sydney, "and see what's really going on here in the forest. I'm sure it's over this way—the direction the mountain man came from. We should be safe now that he's on the other side of the lake."

The girls pushed their way through the brush and the brambles. Before long, they heard the buzzing noise. They followed it.

"Unless something terrible happens, let's agree not to run away," said Sydney.

"Agreed," said Alex.

The noise grew louder. Then finally they saw the familiar purple glow. It was straight ahead of them lighting up the tops of the trees.

"Careful," said Sydney. "Let's go slow." She opened her waist pack and took out the mirrored sunglasses. "I'll put these on in case he comes back."

They walked a little farther until they came to a clearing. They peeked out from the bushes and saw a campsite bathed in the eerie, purple light. There was a campfire ring made of stones, a folding table, and a collection of pots and pans. A bedroll was neatly placed on the table by a small canvas sack. Sydney noticed a seat made from a split-timber log next to the fire ring. "This is where he lives," she said.

"What's that awful smell?" Alexis asked.

"The manure pile," said Sydney. She pointed to a stinking pile of debris at the edge of the clearing. "Now we know where Biscuit was."

Bravely, the girls walked into the campsite.

"The light is coming from over there," said Alexis. "Near

the base of that gnarly old pine tree."

"Let's go check it out," said Sydney.

"Oh Syd, do you really think we should? I feel like we're trespassing or something."

"The forest doesn't belong to him," said Sydney. "It belongs to everybody."

She walked toward the glowing purple light. The buzz grew stronger. The light flashed off Sydney's sunglasses and bounced like prism light across the tree trunks.

"Oh my goodness," said Sydney. "Look at that!"

They were at the entrance to a cave. Its gaping doorway was almost hidden by the low, sweeping branches of an evergreen tree. The purple light came from inside. The buzzing sound echoed from deep within. It ricocheted off the cold, stone walls and sounded like a swarm of angry bees.

Sydney stopped just outside the entrance. She squatted down and tried to look inside. "What do you think is making the purple light?" she asked. "And what's that noise?"

"I don't know," said Alex. "But maybe we shouldn't be here."

"I think we should do some spelunking," said Sydney.

"Some what?" asked Alexis.

"Cave exploring." Sydney explained. She stood and took a few steps into the cave. Then bravely, she took a few steps more. When she did, the buzzing noise stopped.

Suddenly, a great *whoosh* of icy-cold air rushed through the cave. It hit Sydney in the face, sending a chill down to her toes. The buzz turned into a sound that was like a whirling helicopter blade—*whop-whop-whop.*

Out of the noise came a raspy voice whispering, *"Go back! Go back! Go back!"*

The girls turned and ran as fast as they could.

"Alex! Run for your life!" Sydney screamed.

Through the lens of the special sunglasses, she saw something behind them. It was the monstrous dog—the same one that had looked into the bedroom window. It raced after them now, lunging at their heels.

CHAPTER 9

Nice Doggie

Sydney felt the dog's huge front paws wrap around her ankles. She fell to the ground facedown. Then came a *thud* as the animal leaped onto her back. The wind rushed out of her lungs, and she thought for sure that she would die. But then a long, wet tongue licked the side of her face.

"Sydney!" Alexis screamed when she saw her friend lying there helplessly.

The big, black dog lifted its head and looked Alexis straight in the eyes. *Wuf!* Its jowls shook like jelly when it barked.

"Nice doggie," Alexis said, standing still.

Sydney stayed on the ground, not knowing what to expect from the big animal stretched across her back.

"Sydney," Alexis said softly. "I think he's friendly."

She took a few steps toward the dog with her hand extended, palm up. The dog sniffed the air, perhaps wondering if she held a treat.

"Get it off me," Sydney demanded.

"I'm trying," said Alexis quietly. "Nice doggie. Follow

Alex now." She kept her hand extended and took a few steps backward.

The dog stood. Its belly was at least three feet above Sydney's back, and she felt as if she were under a table. As it walked away from her and toward Alex, Sydney noticed its long, gangly legs.

"What *is* this thing?" she asked.

"It's a very nice doggie," Alexis said sweetly as she coaxed the animal to come near to her.

"And it has a head the size of a big pumpkin," she continued, "and spooky brown eyes and sharp teeth, and the closer it gets to me, the more scared I am. But I'm going to save you, Sydney, no matter what. Now, while I'm talking real nice to the doggie and have its attention, why don't you get up very quietly and get out of here? Nice doggie, come here. . . . Nice doggie."

"I'm not leaving you alone with it," said Sydney, getting up on all fours. "We're in this together."

"It's all right," Alexis replied. "I'll be fine." She shivered as the dog's black nose, at least the size of a baseball, thrust into her hand and sniffed. "I wish I had a dog biscuit or something."

Sydney stood up. "I stuck one in my waist pack. Oh my, he's huge!"

Now that she was standing, she could see just how big the dog was. The top of its back was higher than her waist. It had a thick, muscular body, a long tail that curled upward, and short, floppy ears.

"Sydney. . .I think the doggie wants a biscuit *now*," said Alexis. The dog was eagerly licking her hand.

Sydney unzipped her waist pack and found one of Biscuit's dog treats on the bottom.

"Here, dog," she said. "Hungry?"

As soon as the dog saw Sydney pull the biscuit out of her pack, it stopped licking Alexis's hand and rushed toward her. Before Sydney could get out of the way, it stood on its hind legs and plopped its paws squarely onto her shoulders, knocking her backward into a tree trunk. She stood there, pinned between the tree and the dog, its big head looking down at her.

WUF!

"Oh Alex." Sydney gasped. "He's way taller than I am!"

"Maybe you should give him the biscuit," Alexis suggested.

A voice in Sydney's head whispered, *Stay calm. You're in charge. Tell him to get down.*

"Get down!" Sydney said, firmly.

WUF!

"I said, *get down!*" Sydney repeated.

The dog dropped his paws from her shoulders and stood in front of her, looking her straight in the eyes.

"Now, *sit*," she said.

Surprisingly, the dog sat. Sydney tossed the biscuit to him, and he scarfed it down in one big gulp. Then he sat there waiting for another.

"Now what?" Alexis asked.

Sydney took the mini-microcam out of her pack and snapped a quick picture of the animal as it sat there. "I don't know what to do next," she said. "I think this is what we heard howling and barking in the woods. I'm pretty sure its Fang—*his* dog. Let's see how well he follows commands. Fang, *stay!*" she said. The dog didn't move. "Great. Come on, Alex. Let's go."

The girls started to walk. They only went a few yards before Fang got up and began following them.

"Go back!" Sydney commanded.

Fang sat down and whined like a puppy.

The girls started off again, and once more Fang trotted along behind them.

"Sydney, I think we're going to have to take him back to the campsite," said Alexis. "Otherwise, he's going to follow us all the way to the cabin. We can't risk the mountain man discovering that we've been snooping around."

Sydney sighed. "I guess you're right. Come on, Fang. Let's take you home."

The girls turned and walked in the opposite direction, with Fang playfully romping at their side. As they approached the campsite, they were keenly aware that the whooshing noise had disappeared. Once again, the forest was quiet except for the buzzing sound deep within the cave.

"Wait," said Sydney. She stopped in the bushes at the

edge of the clearing. "You stay here with Fang. I'm going to circle around and make sure the mountain man hasn't come back yet."

Fang was happy to have Alexis pet him while Sydney explored the campsite. She made a wide circle around the grounds, careful to stay hidden among the trees. Everything was silent—the mountain man hadn't come back.

Then Sydney made a strange discovery. In the forest floor was a large rectangular-shaped hole covered with a metal grate. When she got closer, she heard the buzzing sound deep inside the earth. A hazy, purple light shined up through the grate and lit the tops of the pine trees nearby. A tall cyclone fence with a gate surrounded the hole, and a big padlock secured the gate. Sydney was curious. She wished that she could get closer and look down through the hole into the earth. Something mysterious was going on down there. She was sure of it.

Sydney was so quiet when she came up behind Alexis and Fang that they didn't hear her. "All clear. He's not there," she said.

Alexis jumped. Fang whirled around, and his lips curled up in a growl.

"Nice doggie!" Alexis exclaimed. Then she said to Sydney, "Don't scare him like that, or me either."

"I'm sorry," Alexis said. "I wasn't thinking. Come on. I found where the light comes from." She led Alexis to the hole in the ground.

"Well, what do you make of that?" Alexis asked.

"I don't know," said Sydney. She took a picture with the mini-microcam. "But I'd love to get a closer look." She handed the camera to Alexis. Sydney put one hand into the wire mesh of the fence, then the other. Carefully, she lifted one foot and stuck the toe of her shoe into the mesh. Then Sydney began to climb.

"No!" said Alexis. "Syd, don't you dare! You don't know who or what's down there. It might be dangerous!"

She grabbed on to Sydney's leg and kept her from climbing any farther.

"Alexis!" said Sydney. "Let go."

"No," Alexis said firmly. "We'll find another way."

Reluctantly, Sydney got down.

Alexis sniffed the air. "Something smells different here," she said. "Did you notice? It smells earthy, like after a spring rainstorm."

"You're right," Sydney agreed. "It smells like wet dirt. Maybe an underground stream flows through the cave."

"But it wouldn't have dirt around it," Alexis countered. "Caves are made of rock."

"You're right again," said Sydney.

The Wonder Watch on Alexis's wrist began to jiggle. MESSAGE WAITING: McKENZIE. A message scrolled across the watch's face. I'M THE ONLY ONE IN THE CHAT ROOM LOOKING AT THESE PICTURES. *WHERE ARE YOU GUYS?* AND WHERE'D YOU GET THE BERNADANE?

Alexis spoke softly into the tiny microphone. "We're sleuthing in the mountain man's campsite in the forest. We saw him row his kayak to the other side of the lake, so he's not here. We found a cave. Near it, there's a hole in the forest floor with a fence around it. What's a bernadane?"

McKenzie's reply flashed on the screen. A BERNADANE IS A CROSS BETWEEN A SAINT BERNARD AND A GREAT DANE. I SAW ONE AT OUR STATE FAIR LAST SUMMER. THEY'RE HUMONGOUS!

"Tell me about it," said Alexis. "The bernadane is standing next to us. His name is Fang, and he's the mountain man's dog. He's friendly. We can't talk now. The mountain man will be back soon, and we have exploring to do. More later."

HIS NAME IS FANG? BE CAREFUL. TAKE LOTS OF PICTURES. AND SHOUT IF YOU NEED US.

The screen went black.

"So, he's a bernadane," said Sydney. "That's comforting. At least he's not part wolf." She reached over and patted Fang on the back of his thick neck.

"Sydney," said Alexis. "You don't think Fang killed that coyote on the beach last night, do you?"

"I've been wondering about that, Alex. But if he did kill it, then why? He doesn't seem like a mean dog. Maybe he was just defending himself."

Fang ran circles around the girls, wanting to play.

"Mr. Lumley saw something big run off into the woods,"

Alexis said. "They thought it was a bear. But think about it, Syd. If you saw Fang running in the dark, you might think he was a bear. He's black and big like a bear. Maybe Fang has a dark side."

Sydney didn't even want to think about that. "Well, right now, we have the problem of getting Fang to stay here so we can go back to the resort. Any ideas?"

"No," said Alexis. "Unless we tie him up."

"If we do that, the mountain man will know that someone was snooping around here," said Sydney.

"That's right," Alexis answered. "But he won't know who it was. I don't know what else we can do, Syd. Otherwise, he'll follow us."

"Let's go inside the cave," Sydney suggested. "Maybe Fang has his own room or something, and we can leave him there."

"But what about that horrible sound we heard and the whispering?"

"I have a feeling it won't hurt us," Sydney told her. "I think the mountain man made it as a trick to scare people away. And since the mountain man is nowhere around, I'm not going to be afraid to go inside."

Sydney and Alexis hurried toward the cave's entrance with Fang romping ahead of them. He trotted inside, and the girls followed. Alexis linked her arm through Sydney's. The only light in the cave came from daylight seeping through the entrance—and it was rapidly fading away.

Ahead of them lay nothing but a faint purple glow.

"Do you remember in *The Wizard of Oz*, how the scary wizard turned out to be Professor Marvel, an ordinary man?" Alexis said. "He was hiding behind a curtain making things work to create a vision of the wizard. It was all done with tricks."

"I remember," said Sydney.

"Well, maybe the mountain man is like that. Maybe he's not scary at all, but a very nice man like Professor Marvel."

They were about a dozen yards inside the cave now.

"Maybe," said Sydney. She stopped and took a flashlight from her waist pack.

"Hey, what's that?" Alexis asked. An old canvas knapsack was propped against one of the cave's stony walls.

Sydney went to check it out. "Shoot! The flashlight batteries are almost dead. I see something written on the knapsack, but I can't read it."

"Hang on a minute," Alexis said. She pulled out her cell phone.

"You'll never get a signal in here," Sydney warned.

"I'm not going to call anybody," Alexis answered. "My phone has a built-in flashlight." She pushed a button on the phone, and the light lit up. She pointed it at the canvas sack.

"J.C." said Sydney. "It's the initials J.C. Are you thinking what I'm thinking?"

"Jesus Christ," Alexis said in almost a whisper.

"No! Although I'm sure Jesus is here protecting us. J.C.,

as in Jacques Chouteau. This thing is old enough to be his," said Sydney. "This must be the cave where he hid his stuff."

"Maybe the mountain man is a thief," Alexis suggested. "Maybe he found Jacques's money and furs in here, and he's selling them for his own profit."

"You might be right," Sydney agreed. She shined the light around the rough, rocky wall. "Check this out," she said, focusing the beam on a series of lines.

"There must be a hundred or more lines carved into this wall," Alexis said. "It looks like someone is keeping score."

"Or keeping track," Sydney said. "Maybe Jacques Chouteau was trapped in here and kept track of the days. Remember? Duncan said that he got trapped in a cave and died there."

"But that's a legend," Alexis told her.

"But maybe the legend isn't a legend," Sydney said. "Maybe the story is true. Jacques Chouteau died here, and the mountain man found his body. Maybe the mountain man has been excavating this site, digging away at the debris from the avalanche and searching for buried treasure. Maybe that place in the woods where we found the shovel is where he buried Jacques!"

"Ewwww, do you think so?" Alexis asked.

Sydney snapped pictures of the knapsack and the etchings on the wall.

Meanwhile, Alexis counted the marks. "One hundred twenty-six," she said. "Do you think Jacques could have stayed alive in here for one hundred twenty-six days?"

"Only if there was a source of air and water," Sydney answered. "If that was the case, then he probably starved to death."

GRRRRRAH, pant, pant. Fang trotted toward them holding something in his teeth.

"What do you have, boy?" Alexis asked. She took a closer look. "He has a bone, Sydney." She gasped. "Maybe it's human!"

Fang dropped the stubby, white bone at their feet.

Sydney inspected it. "It could be from an animal. At least, I hope so. On the other hand, I still wonder what's buried in the forest near those mushrooms we saw?"

"Oh Sydney!" Alexis exclaimed.

Wuf! Wuf! . . . Wuf! Wuf. . .

"I think he wants us to follow him."

Reluctantly, the girls accompanied Fang deeper into the cave toward the purple light. After a few minutes, they entered a small room filled with stalactites and stalagmites. The formations glistened in the neon purple glow.

"Oh, it's beautiful, like an ice castle!" said Alexis.

Fang led them around, sniffing as he went.

"Ack!" Alexis squealed.

A cold drop of water had dripped from a stalactite on the cave's roof onto Alexis's face.

In the corner of the room, they found a door made of thick, wooden planks. Its heavy iron latch was padlocked shut. Cut into the bottom of the door, there was an opening about a foot square. Fang lay down and sniffed it. Then he whined and started digging at it with his paws.

Sydney got on her hands and knees and looked inside. "All I can see is a bright purple light. And it smells really musty in there. I wish I were small enough to climb through this opening, because I think we've found the treasure room."

Alexis got down on the floor, too, and stretched out on her stomach trying to get a better look.

"I can't see anything either," she said. "I think we should go to Tompkins' and chat with the girls. We need to make a plan."

"I agree," said Sydney, standing up. "We need to come back here and find out what's behind this door."

Suddenly, Fang perked up his ears. He cocked his head. Then he raced toward the cave's entrance.

"Oh no," Sydney said. "Trouble. I think the mountain man is back."

"We're trapped!" Alexis gasped, standing up. "Oh Syd! What are we going to do?"

Think positive, Alexis, she said to herself. *Remember Isaiah 43:5: "Fear not, for I am with you." Everything is fine. It's all good. Besides, on all the TV shows and movies, the heroines always get out of the situations just fine.*

"The only way out is through the front door," said Sydney. "Let's go. No, wait!" She took several quick pictures of the door and its mysterious opening. "Now let's go."

They ran toward the cave's entrance. Sydney was prepared to fight the mountain man if she had to. But as they came nearer to the door, they heard Fang barking in the distance. *Baw-wha-wha! Baw-wha-wha!*

"It sounds like he's found something," said Alexis.

"Or some*one*," Sydney suggested.

The girls hurried out of the cave and into the fresh, woodland air. They were relieved that no one was in the campground. But then they heard it—the whistling. The mountain man was back, and he was walking through the forest heading into camp.

Sydney reached into her waist pack and took out the GPS locator. "That way to the resort," she said, pointing north. "Run! We have to get out of here before Fang gives us away."

The girls ran through the forest, back to the resort as fast as their legs could carry them.

The Plan

More visitors had arrived for the weekend, and all of the cabins at Miller's Resort were occupied. Little children splashed in the water near the narrow beach. Moms sat in lawn chairs reading novels, while dads fished in motorboats. Each cabin's dock had at least one young boy fishing. When the girls came running out of the woods, they noticed Duncan fishing on theirs.

"Don't yell at me, okay?" he said when he saw them. "You guys were off somewhere playing, and I didn't think you'd mind if I used your dock."

Sydney debated whether to tell Duncan about the mountain man. She thought he might know something and maybe provide some clues.

"We weren't playing," she said. "We were spying on a guy in the forest."

Duncan looked at her suspiciously.

"There's a guy living in a cave in the forest," said Sydney. "He looks like a raggedy, old mountain man, and he has a gigantic dog. Standing up on its hind legs, it's more than six feet tall. A purple glow comes from the cave, and we discovered a secret room inside, and there are noises— buzzing and whooshing and someone whispering in the trees."

"Ah-ha!" Duncan laughed out loud. "You guys can't fake me out. There's nothing in that forest but a bunch of wild animals."

"No, she's telling you the truth," said Alexis.

"Yeah, right," Duncan replied. "You're not going to scare me off this dock with a ghost story. You just want me to believe you so I'll go look. Then, while I'm gone, you'll fish in my spot. No way!"

Sydney looked at Alexis and shrugged. "Well, we tried," she said. "And by the way, Duncan, this isn't *your* spot. Who's winning the dockside contest, so far?"

"I am," he said. "Thirty-five and a half inches. My fish is on ice at Tompkins'."

"Well, enjoy the lead while you can," Sydney told him. "We have an errand to run, and then we'll be back here to catch the biggest muskie in North Twin Lake."

Duncan laughed. "Whatever," he said. As the girls walked away, they heard him mutter, "Purple glow. It's nothing but the Northern Lights. Dumb girls."

Sydney and Alexis went to Tompkins' Ice Cream Shop. Just inside the front door, they saw Duncan's fish on display in a freezer case.

"You've got to admit his fish is really big," said Alexis. "Do you think we can catch an even bigger one?"

"We're going to try," said Sydney. "Take a look at that monster fish that someone caught from a boat."

A forty-two inch muskie lay next to Duncan's. The tag on it read FRED LUMLEY.

"Well, it looks like both of the Lumleys are in the lead," said Alexis.

"Great," Sydney said sarcastically. "And if they win, Duncan will think for sure that girls can't fish."

"I thought we were going to be nice to Duncan," said Alexis.

"We can be nice and still win the contest. I was reading my Bible last night, and I memorized a verse. Do you want to hear it?"

"Sure," Alexis answered.

" 'You know that many runners enter a race, and only one of them wins the prize. So run to win!' That's what it says in 1 Corinthians 9:24."

"But I don't think the Bible means a fishing contest," said Alexis.

"Well, I think the verse means that God wants us to always try to do our best," said Sydney. "So that's what I'm going to do. I'm going to be nice to Duncan *and* fish to win."

They went to the back of the shop, booted up the computer, and logged on to the Camp Club Girls Web site. Once they got to the chat room, they found the other girls trying to make sense of the pictures Sydney had snapped with the mini-microcam.

Sydney: *We're back at the ice-cream shop.*

Elizabeth: *Thank goodness! We've been praying for your safety.*

Alexis: *We're fine. Got out of the camp just as the mountain man was returning.*

Kate: *I researched Jacques Chouteau. He did exist and disappeared one day. I found tons of legends about him. He's almost as famous in the Northwoods as Paul Bunyan.*

Sydney: *We think the mountain man found the cave where Jacques Chouteau died. That old knapsack inside has Jacques' initials on it. We think Jacques was trapped in the cave, and marked off the days by scratching lines on the wall.*

Bailey: *So that's what those marks are.*

Alexis: *That's what we think. Fang brought us a bone when we were in the cave.*

Elizabeth: *Fang?*

Sydney: *That's what the mountain man calls his dog. Mac says the dog is a bernadane, part Great Dane and Saint Bernard.*

Elizabeth: *I can't believe that picture. He looks huge.*

Sydney: *He is, but he's friendly. When he chased us, he just wanted to play. We wondered if the bone was one of Jacques'.*

Bailey: *Eewwwwww.*

Sydney: *Someone was digging in the forest. We wondered if the mountain man was burying Jacques' bones there.*

Bailey: *Eewwwwww!*

McKenzie: *Why'd you take pictures of mushrooms?*

Alexis: *We found a bunch in the forest. This morning we found a mushroom on the dock and more of them floating in the water. We also found a* Field Guide to Mushrooms *book near the picnic table.*

McKenzie: *What's up with that?*

Alexis: *We don't know, but it seems like more than a coincidence.*

Sydney: *Maybe something evil is happening in that cave. We found a hole in the ground with a locked fence around it. Purple light shines up through the hole. We heard a sound like a helicopter. A cold wind blows, and the trees whisper "go back." And there's a secret room in the cave. We think that's where Jacques kept his treasure.*

Elizabeth: *Syd, trees don't whisper. There has to be a logical explanation. Remember how the land of Canaan was a mystery to Moses and his people? It could have been anything. So Moses sent his guys to check it out, and they discovered something good. I believe behind that secret door, you'll find a logical explanation, and hopefully, a good one.*

Sydney: *I hope you're right, Beth. But how do we get into the room? The door is locked. It has a trapdoor at the bottom that's way too small for Alex or me to get through.*

Bailey: *Can you stick the camera through the trapdoor and take pictures?*

Sydney: *I didn't think of that.*

Kate: *I have a better idea, but first you have to promise me that if you use my idea, the mountain man and his big dog won't be anywhere around.*

Sydney: *We promise.*

Kate: *Okay. Send Biscuit into the secret room with the mini-microcamera strapped to his collar. He's small enough to fit through the trapdoor. You can watch the monitor and see what's inside. But take very good care of him!*

Sydney: *You know we will. That's a great idea, Kate!*

Bailey: *What kind of mushrooms are they?*

Sydney: *I don't know. Why?*

Bailey: *I'm just curious. You usually know stuff like that.*

Alexis: *I'll see if I can find them in the field guide. We'll go back in the woods tomorrow and wait for the mountain man to leave. If he*

> *does, I'll babysit Fang while Sydney takes*
> *Biscuit into the cave.*
> McKenzie: *Sounds like a plan.*

Kate gave instructions for programming the mini-microcamera to send live video to the Camp Club Girls Web site, and Sydney wrote the instructions down. The girls promised to keep in touch.

"Tune in tomorrow," said Alexis. "We'll be broadcasting live from the Chequamegon-Nicolet National Forest."

When they went back to the cabin, Sydney got their poles ready for fishing. In the meantime, Alexis looked through the *Field Guide to Mushrooms*.

"There are tons of pictures in this thing," she said. "I don't know where to look. Wait. I found a list in the back of the book that tells which mushrooms grow in which states. That should be helpful. Let's see. . .Washington, West Virginia. . .Wisconsin! Here it is."

Alexis thumbed through the pages while Sydney got dough balls out of the refrigerator.

"I think I found it," she said. "You're going to love this, Syd. It has the scientific name and everything. The mushrooms that we saw are called *Strobilomyces floccopus*. It means, 'a wooly mushroom that looks like a pinecone.' The common name is the Old Man of the Woods. *Strobilomyces floccopus* only grow in the eastern half of North America, and it says here that you can eat them, but they taste bad."

Sydney checked the minnows swimming in the pail near the kitchen door. "If they taste bad, then why would anyone be digging them up in the forest?"

"That's what I was just wondering," Alexis said. "But I still think that someone was digging up clumps of them where we saw the shovel."

The girls got their fishing gear and headed for the dock. Duncan was still there fishing. He pretended not to see them.

"Duncan, it's time for you to move to your own dock," said Sydney.

Duncan didn't answer.

"Duncan?" Sydney stood there waiting.

"Aw, come on," he said. "Can't we all fish from here?"

Alexis and Sydney sat down on the dock and got their poles ready.

"Why do you have to fish from *this* dock?" Alexis asked. "What's wrong with Dock Two?"

Duncan turned around with a serious look on his face. "Because right out there," he said, pointing, "is the best fishing hole on North Twin Lake. Some of the biggest fish have been caught right there—straight out from this dock. I'm doing some serious fishing here, not just playing around like you girls are. So this is where I should fish." He turned back and sat facing the lake with his legs hanging off the end of the dock. Again, Sydney felt like shoving him in.

Forgive me, God, she prayed silently. *Help me to be nice to him.*

"Duncan," she said. Her voice sounded overly sweet. "You've been fishing here all day. Now, it's our turn. That's only fair, don't you think?"

Duncan sighed deeply. "I guess so," he said. "I'll move." He took his time reeling in his line and packing up his gear. Then he walked to the dock by Cabin Two.

"Maybe we should try spoon lures on our lines," said Alexis. "The fish book says muskies like them. Maybe we can find out where the big ones are swimming."

Sydney caught her breath. "Alex, you just gave me an idea."

"Huh?"

"When you said, 'Maybe we can find out where the big ones are swimming,' it gave me an idea. Why don't we use the mini-microcam? It's waterproof, and if we attach it to the end of one of our lines, we can see where the big fish are. What do you think?"

"I think your idea is *brilliant*," said Alexis, casting her line into the water. "Will you go back to the cabin and get it? And let Biscuit come sit with us. He's been cooped up on the porch all day."

"Will do," said Sydney.

In a little while, she returned with Biscuit trotting at her heels. "Okay, here's what we'll do," she said. "We'll put the camera on the end of your line without any bait or anything. Then you'll cast and slowly reel it in. In the meantime, I'll watch the hand-held monitor here. If we see a big fish, you stop reeling. I'll cast my line as close to yours as I can get it. Then we'll wait for the big one to bite."

"Sounds like a plan," said Alexis. She reeled in her line. "I'm ready." Carefully, Sydney tied the mini-microcam to Alex's line using a Palomar knot.

"I'm glad I took that knot-tying class at camp," she said. "Your fishing line will loop right through this little thingy on the side of the camera and the knot will hold it tight. It's a super strong knot."

With the knot tied and the camera attached, Alexis stood up and cast her line as far into the lake as she could. "Don't look now," she said. "But you-know-who is looking at us." Duncan was on Dock Two watching every move the girls made. He reeled in his line and then cast it near Alexis's.

"Stay clear of my line!" Alexis shouted. "I don't want to get tangled up with you again."

Duncan pretended not to hear.

Sydney loaded a dough ball onto her line. She made sure that it was firmly attached to the hook and double-checked it. The last thing she wanted was for it to fall off if a big fish came along. She turned on the monitor for the mini-microcam. It showed nothing under the water but some green algae.

"Start reeling in your line," she told Alexis. "But go really slow."

Alexis turned the crank on the reel while Sydney watched the monitor. Some small fish swam by—blue gills, sunfish, and perch.

"Nothing but little guys," Sydney said.

Alexis reeled her line closer to the dock. "Do you want me to cast it out again?" she asked.

"Yeah," Sydney answered. "See how far you can throw it."

Alexis stood and took a couple of steps backward.

"Move, Biscuit," she said. "I don't want you in the way."

Biscuit sniffed the wet mini-microcam hanging on the end of the fishing line. Then he sat down and watched Alexis cast the line with all of her might. It arched toward the sky and landed far into the lake.

"All right! Way to go, Alex!" Sydney exclaimed. "That was a great cast!"

She looked at the screen on the monitor in her hand. "Oh my goodness. Look."

She held it in front of Alexis. The camera had landed in the fishing hole—the one where the big ones swam. Several muskies were circling it, probably wondering if it held some food.

"Okay," said Sydney. "Now, I have to cast my line close to yours before they eat the minicam."

She stood and checked the dough ball one last time. It was stuck hard to the hook.

"Wish me luck, 'cause here I go." She stood back, trying to avoid Biscuit. Then with all her strength, she cast her line. It flew through the air and landed with a *splash* just a few yards from Alexis's line.

"All right!" she yelled. "Bull's-eye!"

Duncan watched more avidly than ever.

"Now I guess we just have to wait," said Alexis.

She had barely said the words when the end of Sydney's pole bent sharply toward the water. Then the reel started spinning uncontrollably, unraveling yards of line. Sydney grabbed the pole and held the reel crank to stop it from spinning.

"I've got a big one," she gasped.

Biscuit barked wildly, *Ruff! Ruff! Ar-roof! Ruff! Ruff! Ar-roof!*

That got Duncan's attention. "Need any help over there?" he yelled.

"We're fine!" Sydney shouted.

By now, the other boys on the other docks were watching, too.

For fifteen minutes Sydney fought with the fish. She let it take some line, and then she reeled it in. She kept doing that until the fish was tired out. Then finally, she reeled it up to the dock.

"It's huge!" Alexis cried. She leaned over the edge of the dock and scooped the muskie into the net. It took every ounce of her strength to help Sydney haul it onto the dock.

Biscuit ran to the fish and sniffed it as it lay there flopping.

"Careful, boy. It has sharp teeth," Alexis warned.

The little dog backed away and whined.

Sydney took out the tape measure and measured her catch.

"Thirty-nine inches!" She yelled over to Duncan. "We're heading over to Tompkins' to put it on ice."

A Fungus Among Us

The next morning, the girls quietly prepared for another adventure in the forest. They both knew returning to the mountain man's cave was risky.

"I think we should leave Biscuit here," said Sydney.

"We can't," Alexis argued. "He's the only one who will fit through the trap door."

"I know," Sydney said, as she stuffed their sleuthing equipment into her waist pack. "But if Biscuit barks, he'll give us away. We should go to the campsite alone. Then, when the mountain man leaves, one of us can come back here and get him."

Alexis slipped the Wonder Watch over her wrist. "And what do we do about Fang? If he senses we're nearby, he might run to us or bark or something."

"That's a chance we'll have to take," Sydney said. "We need to be super quiet when we're at the campsite."

Alexis tucked the pepper spray into her pocket just in case they ran into a bear. "Scooby-Doo, where are you?" She sighed as they left the cabin.

"What?" Sydney asked.

"I was just thinking about Scooby-Doo," Alexis explained. "He's always nervous when he goes sleuthing, and I wondered how he would sneak into the campsite."

"Are you nervous?"

"A little," Alexis answered. "Let's check out the mushrooms first and see if anyone has been digging."

When they arrived at the spot where the mushrooms grew, they found them—*gone!*

"Were there hundreds of mushrooms here yesterday or was it all my imagination?" Alexis asked in disbelief.

"They were here," Sydney confirmed. "And now they're not." Someone had dug up the mushrooms, raked the soil, and covered it with dead leaves and pine needles. The shovel was gone, too.

Sydney probed the soil with her foot, looking for clues. "Check this out," she said, pointing to a spot on the ground.

"Ésprit!" said Alexis. "It's the mountain man's boot print! But why would he want so many mushrooms?"

Sydney was busy thinking. "Do you know what, Alex?" she said after a while. "I'm sure he's the one who left the *Field Guide to Mushrooms* on the ground at the resort. And I'm sure, too, that he's responsible for the mushroom we found on the dock and the others floating in the water. And remember, the first night we were here we saw him, and then in the morning the bottom of the boat at our dock was wet, and you noticed a brown, slimy fungus at the edge of the beach."

"That's right," said Alexis. "And mushrooms are a fungus. And that night, after the coyote was killed, we saw the mountain man near our cabin. He was picking at the earth with a stick and putting stuff into a bag."

"Mushrooms!" Sydney added. "Alex, he was searching for mushrooms there in the dark, but why?"

"That's what we have to find out," Alexis said.

They approached the campsite cautiously, stopping briefly when the buzzing noise from the cave turned to the familiar *whop-whop-whop* followed by "Go back! Go back! Go back!"

"I'm not afraid of that anymore," said Sydney. "It's obviously triggered by something we step on or walk by. I think the mountain man is using spooky sounds to keep people away."

"Like the professor in *The Wizard of Oz*," said Alexis.

"Yeah, just like him," Sydney agreed.

They peeked through the bushes at the campsite. The kayak was gone, and so it seemed, were the mountain man and Fang.

"I'm going to check it out," said Sydney. "You stay here." She walked around the campsite, staying well hidden in the brush. She passed the stinking manure pile at the edge of the clearing. Then she went toward the hole in the ground. The purple glow shot up from the hole as it had the day before, and the buzzing noise whirred down below. The fence was still padlocked shut.

"They're not here," Sydney said when she circled back around to where Alexis stood. "Stay put, and I'll get Biscuit."

Sydney sprinted back to the cabin. Biscuit was waiting for her on the screened porch. Before they'd left that morning, Sydney had attached the mini-microcamera to his collar so he'd be ready to go.

"Come on, boy," she said, snapping his leash onto his collar. Biscuit sensed that he was on an important mission. Instead of barking and running playfully into the woods, he sniffed the ground following the trail that the girls had taken. Before long, he led Sydney right to the campsite where Alexis was.

"I have the monitor turned on and ready," Alex said, "and I alerted the other Camp Club Girls that we're about to go in. Kate sent a message that she's worried. I told her we'd make sure Biscuit stays safe."

"Good," said Sydney. "I think only one of us should go into the cave with him."

Alexis said nothing.

"I'll go," Sydney offered.

"I'll stand guard," Alexis said. "And Sydney, be very, *very* careful."

"We will," Sydney promised. Then she and Biscuit walked into the purple glow of the clearing and headed toward the entrance to the cave. Biscuit pulled and strained hard on his leash. He made a gagging, gasping sound as the collar choked him, and he dragged Sydney inside.

"Slow down, boy!" she said. But Biscuit hurried on ahead.

They went through the wide stone-cold corridor toward the secret room, and Sydney noticed that the knapsack was missing—the one with the initials J.C. They rushed past the marks etched on the wall and into the little room with the stalactites and stalagmites. Biscuit seemed to know exactly where he was going. He led Sydney directly to the corner of the room and the locked door. Then he sat and looked at her.

"Are you ready to do some exploring?" Sydney asked him. Biscuit stood on his hind legs and put his paws on Sydney's knees. She reached for the mini-microcam on his collar and switched it on. Video of the outside appeared on the small monitor that Alexis held in her hand. First, the blue denim of Sydney's jeans, then her white sneaker with the lace half tied, then the stone floor of the cave, and finally the wooden planks of the heavy, padlocked door.

"Here we go," Alexis whispered into the face of the Wonder Watch. She took a deep breath and prayed. "Dear God, watch over Biscuit."

"Okay, Biscuit," said Sydney. "You go through this little door and check things out, and be quick about it, too." She unhooked the leash from Biscuit's collar and let him go. He lay down on his fluffy belly and then slithered and squeezed his body through the little trapdoor.

Sydney ran back to where Alexis was so they could

watch the monitor together. "He's in," she said, peeking over Alexis's shoulder.

"So far, all I can see is purple," said Alexis.

"He must be sitting or standing just inside the door," said Sydney. "He's not moving. Why?"

"I don't know," said Alexis. "He's just sitting there."

Suddenly, the monitor went black.

"What's wrong with this thing?" Sydney complained. "We just lost our picture. Wait. . .no. . .I think the camera is taking a picture of something black. Look. Whatever it is, it's moving."

The blackness on the screen bounced up and down and back and forth and then—

"Oh my goodness!" Sydney gasped. A huge, black nose appeared on the screen, sniffing. Then a sparkling, brown eye looked into the camera lens, and a long, pink tongue licked it. "Fang!"

The Wonder Watch jiggled on Alex's wrist. MESSAGE WAITING: KATE. A message scrolled across the screen. THAT'S NOT BISCUIT'S NOSE! WHAT'S IN THERE WITH MY DOG?

Alexis held the watch toward Sydney. "You tell her," she said.

Reluctantly, Sydney pushed the button on the watch and spoke into its face. "Fang is with Biscuit. I had no idea he was in there. But he's friendly, Kate. I'm sure of it."

GET HIM OUT OF THERE THIS MINUTE!

Alexis answered this time. "Kate, we can't. It'll be just fine. I promise. Watch the pictures, and if anything goes wrong, we'll go right in to get him."

PROMISE?

"I promise," said Alexis.

Sydney looked on helplessly. "The only problem with that," she said to Alexis, "is that we *can't* go in and get him. The door is locked."

"I forgot," said Alexis. "So now what?"

"Pray," said Sydney.

"I am," Alexis said. *"I am!"*

The picture on the screen changed to a thick, black tail wagging like a windshield wiper on a car. Then the girls saw all of Fang's behind as he trotted ahead of Biscuit.

"What's that?" Sydney asked.

A long table showed up on the screen. On it were jars of various sizes. Each jar was filled with a clear liquid, and each held a single large mushroom. The mushrooms seemed to glow in the eerie purple light.

"I see labels on the jars, but I can't read them," said Alexis. "It looks like he's handwritten a name and date on each one."

Biscuit must have sensed that the jars were important. He put his paws up on the table and gave them a closer look.

MILLER'S RESORT: 8-1
FOREST: 7-31
WATER'S EDGE: 8-2

138

"Each one has a label telling where the mushroom came from and when he found it," said Sydney. "Look, Biscuit's going into another room."

The purple glow grew softer as Biscuit left the room and entered another. The girls could see Fang running ahead of him.

"It's some sort of laboratory!" said Alexis.

Biscuit sniffed around the room, and the girls saw beakers, bottles, flasks, and test tubes. Some of them had green and pink liquids inside.

There were microscopes and Bunsen burners and magnifying glasses and culture jars.

"Maybe he's a mad scientist," said Sydney.

"Oh," said Alexis. "He's not mad. He can't be! Like Beth said, there's a perfectly logical explanation for all of this."

"Yeah, well. . .then what is it?" Sydney asked, pointing to the monitor screen and ugly gray spores growing in a culture dish.

"I don't know," said Alexis. "He's obviously doing some experiments."

"Obviously," Sydney agreed.

Biscuit wandered past thermometers, trays, tubes, tweezers, scales and stirrers, and blenders and buckets.

"Check that out," said Alexis.

A large beaker sat atop a hot plate. A shimmering green liquid bubbled and boiled inside, and radiant chartreuse steam rose from the top and hung in the air. The beaker came closer and closer as Biscuit moved in to investigate it. He stuck his nose near the steam and jumped back.

"I think maybe he burned his nose," said Sydney.

"Or else it smelled bad," said Alexis. "What do you think the mountain man is cooking?"

"I don't know," said Sydney. "But Biscuit doesn't like it. And have you noticed that Fang is nowhere in sight?"

"I didn't," said Alexis, "but now that you mention it. . ."

WUF!

Alex and Sydney whirled around. There stood Fang. He ran toward the girls and put his big paws on Alex's shoulders, knocking her to the ground. He started licking her face.

"Get him off!" she cried. "Get him off me!"

Sydney reached down and wrapped her arms around Fang's middle. She pulled, trying to lift him off of her friend, but Fang rolled over, pulling Sydney down, too. Soon, the girls were on the ground wrestling with the big, black dog.

"He thinks we're playing with him," Alexis complained. "Fang, no! Fang, stop it! *Sit down!*"

Fang sat. He looked at the girls with sad, brown eyes and cocked his head.

"I think he gets it," said Sydney. She stood and wiped dirt from the seat of her jeans. "Where did he come from? The door to the secret room is locked with a padlock."

A sick look came over Alexis's face. "What if there

are two of them?"

"Two of what?" asked Sydney.

"Two Fangs," Alexis answered, standing up. "Maybe that's another dog inside the cave with Biscuit."

Sydney picked up the monitor that Alexis had dropped when Fang pushed her down. "I don't see another dog," she said, "but where is Biscuit going? Everything is really purple now, and it looks like he's in *another* room." She handed the monitor to Alexis.

Fang sat quietly at the girls' feet.

"I see something," said Alexis.

Biscuit was wandering around a room filled with racks of shallow, dirt-filled trays. As he got nearer to them, the girls saw mushrooms popping out of the soil.

"Alex, there must be thousands of mushrooms in those trays," Sydney said. "Big ones, little ones, all sizes! The room is filled with mushrooms. And do you see that book next to one of the trays? The title says *Cancer Fighting Foods*. I think I know who the mountain man is and what he's doing."

The Wonder Watch jiggled. MESSAGE WAITING: KATE. IT'S A MUSHROOM FARM. WE HAVE THEM IN PENNSYLVANIA. I KNOW ABOUT A BIG ONE IN KENNETT SQUARE. THE MOUNTAIN MAN IS GROWING MUSHROOMS IN THAT CAVE BECAUSE THE CONDITIONS ARE PERFECT: COOL, DARK, AND DAMP.

"You're right," said Sydney. "The cave is a perfect place for a *scientist* to work. I think the mountain man is a scientist, and he's doing some sort of research with mushrooms."

"See," Alexis whispered. "I told you he's not a *mad* scientist. He's a *good* scientist."

You might be right, syd. we learned in class that scientists are experimenting with mushrooms to help sick people. that could be what he's doing. where is Fang? I haven't seen him on the monitor.

Alexis spoke into the watch. "Fang is with us."

How did he get with you if the door is locked?

"We don't know," Alexis told her, leaving out her theory that there might be two dogs.

Something fishy is going on there, and I don't like it. What if we're wrong, and he really is up to no good?

Just then, Fang leapt up and took off running through the forest.

"Oh. Oh," said Sydney. "I don't like this either." Fang's bark echoed through the trees as he ran away from the campsite. "I'm going inside to get Biscuit, and he'd better come when I call him."

Sydney ran to the cave leaving Alexis alone.

"Sydney is going back inside to get Biscuit," Alexis said into the watch. "I think we've seen enough for one day."

Grrrrrrrrrrr. . . . A deep, soft growl came from an alder thicket behind her.

"Fang, is that you?" she asked.

Grrrrrrrrrr. . . . The growl was a little louder now.

"Fang, stop it. You're scaring me," said Alexis. She took a few steps toward the thicket and peeked through its branches.

There, just a few yards away, stood a huge gray wolf. The sides of its mouth curled back, revealing its razor-sharp teeth. *Grrrrrrrrr. . .*

Alexis didn't dare move. She remembered the pepper spray in her pocket, but she was afraid to reach for it. Even the slightest move might make the wolf attack.

Dear God, please help me, she prayed silently.

BAW-WAW-WAW. . . . AR-ROOoooooo. . . . BAW-WAW-WAW!

Fang barreled through the brush and lunged at the wolf, scaring it. The frightened animal ran off through the forest with Fang in hot pursuit.

BAW-WAW-WAW! Baw-waw-waw. . .baw-waw-waw. . .
The barking faded into the distance.

Alexis sighed with relief.

Then, just as her pounding heart was slowing down, she heard—

"Young lady, what are you doing here?"

It was the mountain man! He stood behind her, strong and tall. He held his walking stick and a plastic bag filled with mushrooms. The knapsack, the one with the initials J.C., was flung over one shoulder. Alexis noticed that his bushy, brown beard twitched, and his brow was creased with a frown. His blue eyes flashed. "I asked what you're doing here."

Alexis was trapped. A still, small voice inside told her to be polite. "Hello, sir," she said brightly. "I'm Alexis Howell. Pleased to meet you."

She extended her trembling right hand toward the man.

He reached out and gave it a little shake. "Professor Joshua Cantrell." He introduced himself. "Now, Alexis, what are you doing here?"

Alexis didn't know what to say. She heard herself babbling. "Oh, so you're a professor! We thought you might be a scientist or something. We didn't know for sure, but we figured that you were a perfectly normal person, a very nice man just out here in the woods camping—"

"Little girl, are you lost?" the man asked.

Little girl! Alexis thought. *I'm not a little girl.*

"No, sir," she said. "The truth is our dog is in your cave, and my friend went in to get him."

CHAPTER
12
★ ★ ★ ★ ★

The Secret Revealed

Sydney arrived with Biscuit on his leash.

"Oh. Oh," she said when she saw Alexis with the mountain man.

"So, this must be your friend," Professor Cantrell said. "And I've seen your dog here before. In fact, I took him back to the resort just the other day."

"We know," said Alexis. "We saw you. Sydney, this is Professor Joshua Cantrell."

"You *saw* me?" said the professor. "What are you girls doing this deep in the forest? You shouldn't be wandering out here alone."

Sydney picked up Biscuit and handed him to Alexis.

"A better question, Professor Cantrell, is what are *you* doing here in the woods? We know all about you and your mushrooms."

"You do?" said the professor. "Just what do you know?" He reached over and scratched Biscuit's ears.

"We know that you sneak around in the dark picking mushrooms. We know that you dug up a ton of them in the forest and that you're growing more of them in your cave and experimenting with them. We hope that you're doing something good."

"And that you're not a mad scientist!" Alexis added, wishing that the words wouldn't have slipped from her mouth.

Professor Cantrell laughed. "You're right, I'm a scientist," he said. "And yes, sometimes I get a bit grumpy, but no, I'm not mad."

Wuf! Wuf! Wuf!

Fang shoved his body through the thicket and ran to his master. The professor checked him over.

"Are you okay, boy?" he asked. "That was a good boy for chasing the wolf."

"Wolf?" said Sydney.

"I was almost attacked by a wolf. Fang saved me." Biscuit squirmed in Alexis's arms. "And how did Fang get out of the cave?" she asked the professor. "The door to the secret room is locked."

"Secret room!" said Professor Cantrell. "Have you girls been inside my laboratory? You didn't touch anything, did you?" He was getting irritated now. "How did you get in, and how do you know my dog's name?"

"We've been watching you," said Sydney. "And you can't do anything to us, because right now you're being filmed—live."

"What!" the professor exclaimed, looking around for a

camera. "Young ladies, we need to talk." He invited the girls to sit down on the log near the campfire ring. "Tell me what you know," he said.

Sydney and Alexis explained about being in the forest and seeing the purple glow and hearing strange sounds coming from the cave. They told him about seeing the hole in the ground with the padlocked fence and the old knapsack inside the cave and the marks on the wall. And finally, about their theory that he, somehow, had found Jacques Chouteau's treasure.

"We know you're a scientist who's sneaking around in the woods," said Sydney. "And that must mean that you're doing something wrong."

"Girls, girls, girls," the professor said, scratching Fang's ears. "I'm not doing anything wrong."

They heard a rustling in the brush nearby. Then Aunt Dee and Mr. Miller stepped into the clearing.

"Are you girls all right?" Aunt Dee wailed. "Bailey called me and said a man in the forest kidnapped you! I've been frantic!"

"Hello, Charlie," said Professor Cantrell.

"Hi, Josh," said Mr. Miller.

"You two know each other?" Sydney said.

"We do," Professor Cantrell answered. He hesitated. Then he looked at the girls. "Charlie, can they be trusted?"

"I think so," Charlie Miller answered. "I *know* so!" he added, winking.

The professor took a deep breath and let it out slowly. "Girls, if I tell you a secret, do you promise not to tell anyone, *ever*?"

Alexis switched off the mini-microcamera on Biscuit's collar.

"Wait a minute, Alex," said Sydney. "Can all of *you* be trusted not to tell if *we* share a secret?"

The professor, Aunt Dee, and Mr. Miller all gave their word not to tell.

Sydney explained about the camera and the Wonder Watch and promised that the other Camp Club Girls wouldn't tell if they, too, could hear the professor's story.

"That's quite a gadget," Professor Cantrell said, inspecting the watch. "As long as the other girls promise, I'll tell all of you what's going on."

"You'll have their word," said Sydney. She pushed the button on the watch.

"Girls," she said. "Everything is fine here. This is Professor Cantrell. Listen to what he has to say. All of this is top secret—not to be shared outside of our group, *ever*. Do you absolutely, positively promise never to tell another living soul?"

ELIZABETH: I PROMISE.
KATE: ME, TOO.
MACKENZIE: PROMISE.
BAILEY: DITTO!

Sydney handed the watch to the professor and reminded him to push the button so it would pick up his voice.

He held the watch near his lips. "It's true that I've been out at night picking mushrooms at the resort," said the professor. "Very rare mushrooms grow under the trees near the cabins. They only sprout up from the ground in the dark, and I've been harvesting them secretly. You see, these mushrooms might someday be a cure for certain kinds of cancer."

"Kate was right!" Sydney interrupted.

"I've been growing and synthesizing them, and other mushrooms from the forest, in my laboratory. But for now, I need to keep it all a secret. If the press discovers what I'm doing, they'll be all over the place out here."

"So that's why you've been so sneaky," said Sydney. "It all makes sense now. *Strobilomyces floccopus.* Wow, a cure for cancer right here in the Northwoods!"

Suddenly, the buzzing from the cave turned to a *whoosh,* followed by *whop-whop-whop* and "Go back! Go back! Go back!"

"What about those noises?" Sydney asked. "We keep hearing them coming from the cave."

"I've put two huge fans in the cave," said the professor. "They exchange the air every forty-five minutes to keep the climate controlled. Come on, let me show you." He led the group to the fence and unlocked the padlock.

"This is the exchanger," he said, pointing into the hole in the ground. "One fan blows the air up and out of the cave, and the other sucks fresh air in. I keep it locked up so animals don't get curious and fall down into the fans. If you looked carefully, you'd see six other smaller vents covered with metal grates out here in the forest floor."

Alexis set Biscuit down so he could play with Fang. The two dogs ran off together into the cave.

"The purple light is part of my experimenting," the professor explained. He took off his knapsack and laid it on the ground. "I've found that the cultures I grow from the mushrooms need a special kind of light. With a combination of the purple light and certain chemicals, I'm close to finding a substance that might be the cure."

"That's amazing," said Aunt Dee. "I can understand why you'd want to keep it quiet for now. So, the Millers have known about you living and working here in the woods?"

"Betty and I have known Josh for years," said Charlie Miller. "He spends summers working in the cave and harvesting mushrooms from our property."

Just then, Biscuit came running from behind a stand of pine trees.

"Hey," said Sydney. "Where did he come from? I saw him go into the cave a few minutes ago with Fang."

"I dug out a back door in the mushroom-growing room," said the professor. "Putting a door close to the manure pile made it easier for me to get the trays ready for planting."

Fang trotted out of the cave's entrance. He sniffed the professor's knapsack where it lay on the ground.

"Do you want a treat, boy?" he asked, picking up the knapsack. He opened it and took out two dog biscuits. "Here's one for you and one for your friend."

"So that's your knapsack, then, and not Jacques Chouteau's," said Sydney.

"Jacques Chouteau's! Why would you think it belonged to Jacques Chouteau?" the professor asked.

"Because of the initials J.C.," Alexis responded.

"Oh, goodness, no." The professor laughed. "But I'll tell you another secret, and this is a good one. A cave-in happened way back in the mine, and I think, behind all those rocks might lay the body of poor old Jacques. There are tick marks on the walls just inside the cave. I think Jacques made those, counting off the days that he was trapped inside. When I first discovered the cave, the front entrance was blocked. So I had to dig my way in."

"We thought the same thing about the marks," said Sydney. "Our friend, Elizabeth, said that there was probably a logical explanation for everything, and there is. And Alexis always assumed that you were a nice man."

"Why, thank you, Alexis," said the professor.

Aunt Dee looked puzzled. "Who's Jacques Chouteau?" she asked.

Sydney grinned. "Oh, just some old ghost that haunts the Chequamegon-Nicolet National Forest. I'll tell you about it when we drive home tomorrow."

"Well, you'd better," said Aunt Dee. "I need to know everything about this forest because I just found out that I got the job."

"Oh Aunt Dee, that's great!" said Sydney, hugging her. "I'll miss you living with us in Washington, but how cool is it that I can visit you here all the time. And can Alexis come, too?"

"Alexis and all the other Camp Club Girls," Aunt Dee said. "And tonight we're going to have a long talk about how dangerous it was for you girls to be sleuthing in the woods!"

"Over and out," Sydney said into the Wonder Watch. "We'll head for Tompkins' in a little while and chat online."

BETH: OVER AND OUT.
KATE: OVER AND OUT.
MACKENZIE: OVER AND OUT.
BAILEY: DITTO!

They left Mr. Miller and the professor talking about the wolf that killed the coyote on the beach.

"Well, that's another mystery solved," Sydney said as they walked through the woods.

"You girls and your detective work," Aunt Dee complained. "One of these days, you're going to get yourselves into trouble, and then what?"

"Then the Camp Club Girls will come and rescue us," Sydney replied. "But, for now, Alex and I have some fishing to do."

When they got back to the resort, Duncan was fishing on Dock Two.

"Catch anything?" Sydney yelled to him.

He ignored her.

Alexis took out her cell phone and punched in the number for Tompkins' Ice Cream Shop. Then she texted the word FISH. In a few seconds, her phone rang. "Thirty-nine inches," she said. "We're still in the lead."

"Awesome!" Sydney exclaimed. "And I plan to keep it that way. Let's get our poles."

Biscuit pulled and strained against his leash. Sydney bent down to set him free.

"No," said Aunt Dee. "You need to keep him on the leash. Otherwise, he'll run right back to the campsite to play with the professor's dog."

"You're right," Sydney agreed. "Sorry, Biscuit."

In a few minutes, Sydney and Alexis were on their dock fishing. This time, they knew where to cast their lines.

"I sort of feel bad that we're beating Duncan," Alexis said as she sat on the end of the dock with her bare feet dangling in the water.

"You do?" said Sydney. "Why?"

"I don't know," Alexis answered. "Something about him is just so sad."

"Sad!" Sydney exclaimed. "He's a bully." She reeled in her line and cast it out again.

"That's not a very Christian attitude, Sydney. Remember what McKenzie always says, 'Mad is usually a cover up for sad.' She might be right. Mr. Miller said that Duncan doesn't have many friends."

"Yeah, and I can tell you why," Sydney answered.

"We promised to be nice to him," Alexis continued. "I mean, look over there. Boys are fishing on every dock, and none of them seem to know Duncan. You'd think that since he and his dad come here every summer he'd know some of the kids and hang out with them." She reeled in her line just a little.

"Maybe they're first-time visitors, like we are," said Sydney.

"Maybe," Alexis said. "And maybe not." She fished silently for a while. "I'd be really sad if my mom and sister died in an accident," she continued. "He's gotta be sad, Sydney. You don't just forget about something like that."

"You're right," Sydney answered. "But, Alex, I really want us to win this contest. If we don't, he's going to think that girls can't fish. If nothing else, I want him to learn that he's wrong about that."

The tip of Alexis's pole bent down. She grabbed tight to the reel and started turning the crank. "I don't think it's very big," she said. "It doesn't feel like the other fish we caught."

Duncan watched them from his dock.

Alexis reeled in her line and found a small sunfish dangling from the hook. Carefully, she removed the hook and set the fish free.

"Ah-ha-ha!" Duncan laughed loud enough for the girls to hear. "Nice one, Alex," he called to them. "That'll win the prize for sure."

"See what I mean?" said Sydney.

Just then, Duncan's pole jerked in his hands. He stood up and pulled back, setting the hook in the fish's mouth. Then he tried to reel it in. The fish was strong, and it put up a gigantic fight. While the girls watched from their dock, Duncan pulled hard. He let the fish run with the line. Reeled it in. Let it run. Reeled it in, again and again. The fish kept fighting. Duncan pulled and yanked and reeled, but he made little progress.

"Do you think we should go help him?" Alexis asked.

"Goodness no," said Sydney. "He'd never accept our help anyway."

Then it happened—something the girls could never have imagined. They heard Duncan scream, "Ah-ah-yeeeeeahhhh!" The scream was followed by a humongous *splash!* The strength of the fish pulled Duncan right off the end of the dock and into the water.

The girls' first instinct was to laugh. There he was, soaking wet, thrashing around near the dock. Sydney saw his pole in the water, flying toward them. She reached down and grabbed it. Alexis set her pole on the dock and grabbed Sydney's ankles just in time, or she would have been thrown into the water, too.

Sydney managed to get herself upright. Then, just like Duncan, she fought the fish with all of her might.

"Help me! Help me!" Duncan screamed. "I—I c–can't sw–swim!"

The other boys didn't notice, or they didn't care.

"Oh my!" Sydney gasped. She handed her pole to Alexis, and then she sprinted to Duncan's dock.

She jumped into the water, wearing all of her clothes, and grabbed hold of Duncan's shirt just before his head disappeared under the water. He sputtered and spit and flogged around.

"Duncan, calm down!" Sydney demanded. "You're fine."

She pulled him to the side of the dock into shallow water.

"Put your feet down. You can reach the bottom now."

Duncan did as he was told, and the two of them walked up onto the shore.

By now, everyone on the docks was watching. "Everything all right?" a boy shouted from Dock Three.

Duncan stuck his hand in the air and waved him off.

"How come you embarrassed me like that?" he said to Sydney. "All the guys are lookin' at me now."

"Embarrassed you!" Sydney said, standing there dripping wet. "If I hadn't *embarrassed* you, you'd be dead!"

Duncan hung his head.

"I'm sorry," he whispered. "I guess you saved my life."

"Hey! Hey! Come here!" Alexis shouted from Dock One. She'd managed to reel the big fish in. "I need someone to net this monster."

Sydney and Duncan hurried over to help her. It took all three of them to pull the muskie up onto the dock. The fish's gaping, tooth-filled mouth swung open and shut as it still fought against the hook. Sydney took out her tape measure and measured it.

"Forty inches," she announced.

Duncan stood there red faced. "Well," he said. "I guess you guys won. The contest ends in an hour, and I'm done fishing."

Alexis wiped her wet hands on her jeans. "What do you mean, Duncan? You won," she said. "You did all the work. I just helped you to pull it in."

Duncan's face brightened.

"Do you mean it?" he said. "I won?"

"It's your fish," said Sydney. "Congratulations." She put her hand out, and Duncan shook it. "There's just one thing," she said.

"What's that?" Duncan asked suspiciously.

"I want you to say that *girls can fish* and mean it."

Duncan looked down at the dock. "Girls can fish, I guess."

"You guess?" said Alexis.

"Naw," he replied. "Girls *can* fish."

157

When Duncan's dad heard about Sydney rescuing Duncan from the water, he insisted on treating them and Aunt Dee to supper at The Wave Restaurant. As it turned out, Duncan and his father were good company. Mr. Lumley knew a lot about the lake, and he seemed eager to find out more about Aunt Dee's job as a forest ranger.

"I had fun tonight," said Alexis, as she and Sydney got ready for bed. "Duncan and Mr. Lumley turned out to be all right."

Sydney sat on her bed reading her Bible. "They did," she agreed. "Alex, isn't it strange how sometimes you can read the Bible and it seems to speak to you about what's going on right now? Do you want to hear the verse I just read?"

"Sure," Alexis answered.

"I found it in Leviticus 19:18," said Sydney. "It goes like this. 'Do not seek revenge or bear a grudge against one of your people, but love your neighbor as yourself.' Duncan's not the only one who learned a lesson this week. I learned that revenge isn't good. During supper tonight, I realized that Duncan might have been a friend. We could have had fun hanging out with him all week."

"Well," said Alexis. "Maybe next summer. With your aunt working here, you can come back anytime."

"That's true," said Sydney.

Darkness had fallen on the Wisconsin woods. Sydney reached across her bed to shut the curtains on the window. A dark, shadowy figure moved about near the beach.

"Professor Cantrell is out there searching for mushrooms," she said.

Alexis climbed into Sydney's bunk and looked.

"No, Syd," she said. "It's not the professor. Look again. It's a bear! Isn't that cool?"

"Cool?" Sydney asked. "I thought you were afraid of bears."

"I was," said Alexis. "But after what we've been through this week, a big, old bear doesn't scare me at all."

Join the Camp Club Girls online!

www.campclubgirls.com

❃ Get to know your favorite Camp Club Girl in the Featured Character section.

✳ Print your own bookmarks to use in your favorite Camp Club Book!

✳ Get the scoop on upcoming adventures!

(Make sure to ask your mom and dad first!)